DISAGREEABLE TALES

DISAGREEABLE TALES

LÉON BLOY

TRANSLATED BY ERIK BUTLER

WAKEFIELD PRESS   CAMBRIDGE, MASSACHUSETTS

Originally published as *Histoires désobligeantes* in 1894
This translation © 2015 Wakefield Press

Wakefield Press, P.O. Box 425645,
Cambridge, MA 02142

This book was set in Garamond Premier Pro
and Helvetica Neue LT Pro by Wakefield Press.
Printed and bound in the United States of America.

ISBN: 978-1-939663-10-8

Available through D.A.P./Distributed Art Publishers
155 Sixth Avenue, 2nd Floor
New York, New York 10013
Tel: (212) 627-1999
Fax: (212) 627-9484

10 9 8 7 6 5 4 3 2 1

CONTENTS

TRANSLATOR'S INTRODUCTION
THE GOSPEL OF THE GUTTER

No one can be an atheist who does not know all things. Only God is
an atheist.
—Flannery O'Connor

Man is profoundly dependent on the reflection of himself in another
man's soul, be it even the soul of an idiot.
—Witold Gombrowicz

A quick look at the writings of Léon Bloy (1846–1917) suggests that the author numbered
among the host of fin-de-siècle French authors who delighted in transgression and the
obscene. Such an impression is hardly wrong. Bloy's narratives feature theft, onanism,
incest, murder, and a wealth of other perversions, and they are served with gusto befitting
the most decadent of literary blackguards. At the same time, however, the filthy feast is
not for the senses alone, for it is redolent of spiritual mysteries. More than any of his peers,
Bloy knew that the wellspring of religion is crime against man, nature, and God. No scientific progress, social engineering, or secular pragmatism could ever explain the human
capacity for evil—much less control it.

Like his contemporary Nietzsche, Bloy knew he was out of step with the times.
Unlike the German philosopher—who stared into the sun and declared himself the Anti-
christ—Bloy sounded the abyss and found the Father, the Son, and the Holy Ghost. The
second of six sons born to a freethinking yet stern father and a pious Spanish-Catholic
mother in southwestern France, Bloy nourished antireligious sentiments in his youth. His
outlook changed radically when he moved to Paris and came under the influence of Jules-
Amédée Barbey d'Aurevilly (1808–1889)—the unconventionally religious novelist best
known for *Les Diaboliques*, a collection of narratives about women whose criminal acts
represent a delicate *pas de deux* of the sacred and the profane.

Bloy embraced Catholicism and devoted himself to the holy life. How he did so admits little comparison with anyone else in nineteenth-century France—or, for that matter, the modern world in general. To find the author's spiritual contemporaries, one must look back to the Middle Ages, if not earlier. Bloy's peers are the desert fathers and martyrs of early Christianity, who reveled in torments and trials that a secular age deems morbid and perverse. Flaubert may have written *The Temptation of Saint Anthony*, but Bloy practically lived it. An anchorite of the metropolis, he embraced poverty and self-mortification as complete as the rigors endured by any ancient hermit, often subsisting only on what others grudgingly gave him.

By a law as ancient as the Bible, which says that the elect will be blessed if they follow the Lord and cursed if they do not, our author earned the right to fulminate as fiercely as any prophet against the world that surrounded him. As Caïn Marchenoir, his alter ego in the 1887 novel *Le Désespéré* (and in some of the tales in the volume at hand), Bloy heaped imprecation upon a society that failed to realize the utopia dreamed up by modern revolutionaries—and which stood even farther away from the age-old ideal of Christian brotherhood. The "ungrateful beggar" and the "pilgrim of the absolute," as he came to be known, spared absolutely no one. His vision barely allows for degrees of guilt. But for the mercy of an inscrutable Deity, all mortals would stand condemned.

At the same time, Bloy's intentions are never transparent. It is easy to be led astray by his ranting and invective. His abuse is so florid and detailed that one often fails to realize he is practicing a diversion in order to attack on another front. Thus, his pamphlet *Salvation through the Jews* (1892) trades in same anti-Semitic caricatures that reached a fevered pitch in the notorious Dreyfus Affair (which occurred two years later). As is his wont, Bloy gathers together the foulest hyberbole—and then augments and escalates it. *Salvation through the Jews* provokes and offends, but the author does not mean to join the chorus of bigoted persecutors of the ancient faith. Instead, his purpose is to confound his gentile brethren. If Jews deserve contempt, how much more do their accusers merit chastisement and correction? As (nominal) Christians, they must acknowledge the holiness of both Testaments. This means they are supposed to bow before Christ, who did not "come to destroy, but to fulfill"[1] Jewish law. Ultimately, anti-Semites are hoisted by their own petard: their very logic undoes them. Ever exposed to the rigors of "walking with the Lord," Bloy spread the Gospel like the plague—joyfully wounding the vainglory and pride of those who did not recognize that they, too, had a cross to bear.

Walter Benjamin, the German-Jewish Marxist whose background and overall cultural orientation could scarcely have been more different than our author's, knew as much. He particularly esteemed Bloy's *Exegesis of the Commonplaces* (1902)—a book that, in a contemptuous aside directed at university pedants, recommends establishing a chair for the unpracticed art of "reading between the lines."[2] Here, Bloy affirms the gold standard of proverbial wisdom (for example, "Business is business," or "All roads lead to

Rome") by treating everyday sayings as coins that have passed between so many impure hands that they have lost the value they once held. The parties to blame for the Great Depression of Spirituality (as it were) belong to the hated bourgeoisie, the bugbear of reactionaries and revolutionaries alike. From Bloy's backward-looking standpoint, the ascendancy of the middle classes through manufacture and money made a mockery of the sublime hierarchy that once had united subjects under Church and Crown. At the other end of the political spectrum, Benjamin deplored the same state of affairs with a different point of emphasis: the alienated urban proletariat toils to no end for new feudal lords of commerce who do not even pay lip service to the duties their aristocratic forebears at least pretended to honor. One man looked to the past, the other to the future. Both were dissatisfied with the present (to put it mildly).[3]

Disagreeable Tales appeared in 1894, eight years before Exegesis of the Commonplaces. The collection proceeds in similar fashion, but in the framework of anecdotal narratives. Often, a title will serve as a punch line that comes back at the story's end or, alternately, as an affirmation the narrative as a whole calls into question. Like Charles Baudelaire's poems in prose (e.g., "Let's Kill the Poor"), the collection delivers so many blows to smug self-certainty, widely held opinions, and received ideas. On this score, Bloy shares a predilection for shock with Villiers de l'Isle-Adam (1838–1889), the author of Cruel Tales, and Isidore Ducasse (1846–1870), the self-styled "Comte de Lautréamont." These writers belong to a private pantheon of poètes maudits and "unmodern" artists. Needless to say, Bloy's nods to contemporaries he esteems—the "newly elect of eternity"[4]—are paired with more elaborate (and obscene) gestures to parties he abominates.

Bloy's view of nineteenth-century France is every bit as grotesque as Dante's perspective on fourteenth-century Italy in Inferno. Bloy's "good guys" are like the devils that inflict perpetual punishment on the damned in Dante's poem. But if the medieval author reserved torment for the wicked after death,[5] his modern counterpart portrays Hell on Earth. The characters parading in Disagreeable Tales drag their carcasses through life as if they already occupied the deepest pits of the abyss. Hence the pitch-black humor of the work. Bloy may be likened to a chronicler perched in the stormy clouds of the Apocalypse who can see mortals' disloyalty, impiety, and double-dealing for what they really are—and as soon as they occur. Bloy's language does not mince words, but offers the portrait of realities that people who are not gifted with second sight cannot even discern.

In the unchanging—that is, the eternal—realm of Truth, no exaggeration is possible, no ink too black, and no hue too bold. Being, not seeming, stands at issue. The Sun falls from a right angle on high. "Our souls could see each other. There was the sensation of standing face to face at the edge of a cliff,"[6] cries one of the lost. All that belongs to the passing world must disappear in the light of revelation, and Bloy understands himself as its agent. He takes the "Art for art's sake" of his Symbolist contemporaries and restores it to the Deity whom unbelievers (whether positivists, socialists, aesthetes, or some other incarnation of human absurdity) claim to have dethroned. It is impossible to trump this rhetorical gesture, for it occurs in the name of ages and generations reaching back to the very foundation of the world. Bloy obtains absolute license to attack whomever he wishes—including supposed votaries of the Church, whose failings the "Grand Inquisitor" attacks with special glee.[7]

The ill-mannered apostle delivers his sermons *de profundis*—"from the depths." Bordellos, sewers, and charnel houses are just as cavernous as any site of myth, biblical or otherwise. But the deepest chasm lies in men's—and women's—souls. One of the words recurring with the greatest frequency in *Disagreeable Tales* is "imbecile." This universal affliction consists, above all, in failing to see that the same laws that held in the ancient world are just as true now as they ever were. The benighted mortals who wander about stealing, fornicating, and killing are, each and every one of them, stand-ins for their primal parents, who were dumb enough to take the advice of a talking snake. God once saw fit to do away with the human race; now, humankind breeds and perpetuates its stupidity only because the Creator suffers their idiocy. Nietzsche—notwithstanding all fantasies of assuming a position "Beyond Good and Evil" as a "Prelude to a Philosophy of the Future"—has met his match in Bloy, who enlists metaphysical assistance from the one, true Superman.

Disagreeable Tales proves disagreeable only if one is invested in the depravity it depicts. If not, one can see Bloy for what he is: a crusader brandishing the cross and fighting hellfire with hellfire. The volume at hand has retained the understated title by which the collection has come to be known. In fact, however, *Histoires désobligeantes* might be more properly be rendered *Offensive Tales*, or even *Hurtful Tales*. The writer means for them to sting and scourge—like so many lashes of holy chastisement. The writer knows he is misunderstood and hated for "vampiric excursions"[8] that seek out all that is corrupt and sinful in the modern world. But like any "monster," he can exist only under favorable conditions. Marchenoir and his tales mirror a society that is itself monstrous. The author and his alter ego are in fact among the gentlest inhabitants of the fallen realm. Although Bloy "must *injure*,"[9] he does so through words alone.

As with any literary work, it helps to know something about the author's life and times. This is certainly true of Bloy, who possessed vast (and highly idiosyncratic) erudition, making numerous references both to private readings and to public events in oblique fashion. At the same time, the commentary one might provide would quickly exceed what space allows; inasmuch as our author takes aim at human *types* when he names names, glosses are unnecessary: there are plenty of people walking the Earth today who match the description. In the interest of readability, notes have been omitted; the wonders of the oracular Internet should offer sufficient illumination to the curious. A brief sketch of the age will aid navigation.

A few years after Bloy's birth, in 1851, Louis-Napoléon Bonaparte staged the coup apropos of which Karl Marx, glossing Hegel, made the famous observation that historical events occur twice: "the first time as tragedy, the second as farce."[10] The less-than-great man's reign, which began with harshly repressive measures and, ten years later, introduced the so-called Liberal Empire, was imposing but hollow. The "real" Napoleon had been a revolutionary general who succeeded in conquering half of Europe. Napoleon III, as his nephew called himself,[11] measured up only in appearance. On the one hand, he redesigned the main arteries and public spaces of Paris and other major cities, expanded the railways, modernized the banking system, reformed the educational system, and doubled colonial holdings. But his bluster blew apart when he led France, without any allies, against Prussia in 1870. The war was over in less than a year.

After Napoleon III suffered ignominious defeat at Sedan in September—and on the first day of battle, at that—a republican government took charge of the doomed war. Radicals, however, refused to recognize the new regime, and for some six weeks in the spring of 1871, the Paris Commune controlled the capital. On 21 May, the *semaine sanglante* began when the state marched on its own people. The Third Republic was christened by the slaughter of thousands of Frenchmen by their brethren; even more were taken prisoner and exiled. In a word, the so-called *Belle Époque* during which Bloy did most of his writing was not quite so beautiful for everyone. In 1914, even greater catastrophe befell France and European Christendom in general.

In the roughly one hundred years since Bloy's death, humankind has not improved. Peace in Western and Central Europe was bought at the price of the Second World War, when the powers that had ruled the nineteenth century forfeited their leadership to the Russians and Americans. The Jews were either killed or forced to emigrate. Overseas colonies achieved political (if not economic) independence. For the last few decades, secular society has not managed to produce even the middling pathos of 1950s existentialism or the passing intoxication of 1960s radicalism. Minimally supported by the vestiges of the welfare state or, alternately, lulled (and often medicated) into dull contentment, the occupants of the postmodern aquarium drift in the tepid waters of "the best of all possible worlds." Nothing guarantees this state will last.

One day, the inspired misanthrope will be humanity's consoler. Bloy shows strange compassion for the wretches whose botched lives he portrays. They are the lepers Christ healed and the prostitutes with whom the Son of Man consorted—even the tormentors who finally saw to it that he died. "Father, forgive them; for they know not what they do,"[12] said Jesus. Bloy was only a mortal, and so his mercy cannot be perfect. All the same, he is generous enough to admit what too many still deny: that even (and especially) the worst have a soul. May his overwrought tales remind readers just how terrible it will be when "the last shall be first, and the first last," on that awful day when the "wrath of the Lamb"[13] visits the Earth.

*   *   *

Idiosyncrasies of capitalization correspond to the edition published by Mercure de France (1914). Thanks to Keith Leslie Johnson for feedback on an initial version of the translation—and, of course, to Kimberly Jannarone for charming companionship in darkness and light.

NOTES

1. Matthew 5:17 KJV.
2. Léon Bloy, *Exégèse des Lieux Communs* (Paris: Payot & Rivages, 2005), 298. Cf. Walter Benjamin, Letter to Gerhard (Gershom) Scholem, 16 September 1924, in *The Correspondence of Walter Benjamin, 1910–1940*, trans. Manfred R. Jacobson and Evelyn M. Jacobson (Chicago: University of Chicago Press, 1994) p. 250.
3. Cf. Walter Benjamin, "Critique of Violence," in *Reflections: Essays, Aphorisms, Autobiographical Writings*, ed. Peter Demetz (New York: Schocken, 1986), pp. 277–300.
4. Bloy, "It's Gonna Blow!"
5. With occasional exception; cf. *Inferno* 33, 121–126.
6. Bloy, "Jocasta on the Streets."
7. Bloy, "Cain's Luckiest Find"; cf. "The Religion of Monsieur Pleur," which eulogizes a universally reviled miser who is infinitely more generous than the nominal servants of God, both lay and ordained.
8. Bloy, "The Voluntary Fanatic, or The Conspiracy of Silence."
9. Ibid.
10. Karl Marx, *The Portable Karl Marx*, ed. Eugene Kamenka (New York: Viking, 1983), p. 287.
11. The short-lived "Napoleon II" (1811–1832), the son of Napoleon Bonaparte, was only ever the titular "Emperor of the French."
12. Luke 23:34.
13. Revelation 6:16; Matthew 20:16.

DISAGREEABLE TALES

To my dear friend

EUGÈNE BORREL

In pious memory of Our Lady of Ephesus, who brings us so far away from the filth of the present.

L. B.

The Voluntary Fanatic, or
The Conspiracy of Silence

"We were taught in our childhood," Apemantus told me, "that there are *ten parts of speech*. The profound grammar of the future will declare silence to be the eleventh and most formidable part—the one charged with consuming the rest, as Aaron's serpent devoured the other snakes.

"The commonplace about 'eloquent silence' isn't silly, you know, and 'silence of the passions' should be feared more than the worst talkativeness. 'Conspiracy of silence,' another commonplace, may not be chivalrous, but there's no question it works for killing a man of higher station, one who cannot be dishonored. It's the desert of the vast steppes surrounding the conqueror, which make him die of starvation. It's the infinite solitude of God Himself, of which no one speaks—or wishes to hear spoken.

"Does anyone remember the prodigious devastation of Saint Pierre in Martinique? In thirty seconds, the *silent* breath of a nearby volcano annihilated thirty thousand human beings.

"You told me, Marchenoir, that your daughter took communion for the first time at that very moment; the innocent girl required not a victim less so that her prodigious action would be marked, indelibly and in altogether singular fashion, by a colossal gesture of Death. That's how you, in your dreadful concentration, explain the events of this world! I believe you're right, a thousand times over; still, the abyss is a marvel.

"When the little girl before your own received the Body of Christ, an entire people was alive; . . . when the turn came for the one after her, it was all over for them. *Custodiat animam tuam . . .* These words had sufficed. No more banks, no more stores, no more courts, no more offices of commerce or of love—not even the churches were left. Fifteen hundred leagues away, all at once, they were dead, a dead city, Silence.

"But did you know that one man was saved—*just one*—and that this same party had been CONDEMNED TO DEATH? Others were gladdened, I suppose, at the prospect of witnessing his execution; it was all the rage in distinguished families; no doubt they awaited his torments impatiently. Yet he alone witnessed the masses being put to death! . . .

"Perhaps you think I'm offering you a parable. Well, no. You yourself are the condemned man. You were to be executed by silence. Instead, you have been made the solitary habitant of a silent necropolis."

"My dear Apemantus," I replied, "I should like to believe you're not rattling off some parable, yet it seems you're in the grip of a strange mono-mania. You wish, at all costs, that I be persecuted, and you fail to see that it's quite the contrary: I am the persecutor. Ask our peers. Everyone will tell you that I'm a monster, that there's no way to escape my ferocious jaws. Even if they pet me, wreathe me in flowers, whisper the sweetest things in my ear, give me money and dainty morsels, it's just no good. Saint Martha herself would despair of taming so fierce a *tarasque*.

"I admit that it lies outside my power to remain calm. When I'm not killing, I must *injure*. Such is my destiny. I'm fanatically ungrateful. Because I'm not blind, I can see quite clearly that the whole world is very good; from lily-white purities down to the most notorious brutes, it's just a question of who loves me most tenderly—and will prove as much by presenting the worthiest offerings. There would be no end if I recounted the painstaking care, the attentive concern, and the impassioned pronouncements of which I am ever the object—to say nothing of many heroic sacrifices I have repaid, shamefully and abominably, with only the blackest of schemes. What do you want? I'm a voluntary fanatic.

"You might object that they've been trying to starve me for thirty years—and that by this means two of my children were killed. Since I have no heart, I came to terms with it and showed admirable composure. But all the same, I'm a just man, so I can put myself in the position of those good souls—to whom I owe everything. Their intentions were so upright and pure!

"True, they foolishly thought that silence would kill me. That's trying to poison a crocodile with toad stew. It only made me—and my teeth—stronger. And so, without meaning to do so at all, they've been my benefactors. Silence, poverty, and dreadful sorrow were just what I needed to become an invincible monster.

"The last words you said prove you understand. So why speak to me of starvation and the desert? I've never been so well looked after, nor have I ever flourished so greatly. Silence is a favorable meadow for the ruminants of Eternity; the lush pasture draws the most agreeable creatures to my side almost every day. When silence no longer surrounds my person, it will surely be a terrible day. I shall find myself upon silver manure, on which the lovely daisies and Easter anemones of Pain no longer bloom, and my dispirited companions will run off to graze upon the unicorns' lotus on the mountain.

"So don't worry, Apemantus. The *conspirators* of silence—the *silentarii*, as one would say in Byzantium—are nothing but poor bailiffs who are mistaken when they think they have a noisy troublemaker in me. You've been my guest on many occasions, and you know my jaws move quietly. Even my laugh—when I devour my peers—would not bother a spider weaving; my steps make still less noise, when I stroll between their graves. If they were smart, they'd sound the bell night and day, to warn of my presence and deprive me of the anonymity that smiles upon my vampiric excursions.

"Speak to me no more of these imbeciles."

LÉON BLOY
Bourg-la Reine, November 1913

I. Herbal Tea

Jacques thought himself simply horrible. It was despicable to stay there, in the dark, like some sacrilegious spy while this woman, utterly unknown to him, made her confession.

But then, he would have had to leave right away, as soon as the priest in the surplice joined her—or at least to make a little noise, so they would be aware of a stranger's presence. Now it was too late, and the terrible indiscretion could only grow worse.

Idle and seeking, as wood lice do, a cool place at the end of this scorching day, he had conceived the notion (so little in keeping with his ordinary fancies) of entering the old church; he had seated himself in a dark corner, behind the confessional, to daydream while watching the great rose window disappear.

After a few minutes—knowing neither how nor why—he had become the altogether unwilling witness of a confession.

True, the words didn't reach him clearly; all in all, the only thing he heard was whispering. But toward the end, the exchange seemed to intensify.

A few syllables came loose here and there, emerging from the opaque river of penitential chatter, and the young man—who by some miracle was the opposite of a complete boor—was really and truly afraid of the shocking admissions, which clearly were not meant for his ears.

Suddenly, what was ordained occurred. A violent whirl seemed to start. The immobile waves rumbled as they split apart, as if to make way for a monster. Gripped by terror, the hearer caught impatient words:

"I'm telling you, Father, I put poison in his tea!"

Then, nothing. The woman, whose face could not be seen, rose from kneeling and silently disappeared into the thicket of shadows.

As for the priest, he moved no more than a corpse; long minutes passed before he opened the door and departed with the heavy step of a man shocked by a blow.

It took the incessant chiming of the beadle's keys and the order to leave, long since bellowed in the nave, for Jacques to rise, too—so greatly was he stunned by those words, which echoed noisily within him.

He had recognized his mother's voice perfectly! Oh! There was no mistaking it. He even recognized her walk when the woman's shadow had risen two steps away.

But then, how! Everything collapsed—it all disappeared; it was nothing but a monstrous joke!

He lived alone with this mother; she saw almost no one, and she never went out—except to attend services. He was accustomed to worshiping her, with all his soul, as the paragon of rectitude and kindliness.

As far back into the past as he could see, there was nothing murky, nothing crooked—no exception, not a single deviation. A neat, white road led to the horizon under a pale-blue sky, for the poor woman's life had been quite melancholy.

Since her husband's death at Champigny (which the young man could hardly recall), she had dressed in mourning, devoting herself exclusively to the education of her son, whom she never left for a single day. She hadn't wanted to send him to school, fearing the company he might fall into; so she took his instruction upon herself and built his very soul from pieces of her own. From such guidance, he had acquired an anxious sensibility and singularly delicate nerves; they made him susceptible to ridiculous pains—and perhaps to real dangers, as well.

When the boy entered adolescence, his pranks, which she could not prevent, had made her a little sadder, but her sweetness did not change. Neither scolding nor silent dramas had occurred. Like so many other women, she accepted the inevitable.

In sum, all the world spoke of her with respect, and he alone—the only one to do so, he, her adored son—now saw himself forced to despise her: to despise her on bended knee and with tears in her eyes, as the angels might despise God if He didn't keep His promises!...

Truly, it was maddening—a matter to send one off screaming into the street. His mother! A poisoner! It was insane, absurd a million times over; it was absolutely impossible, and yet it was certain. Had she not just said so herself? He could have torn his head from his shoulders.

But the poisoner of whom? Good God! No one of his acquaintance had died of poison. It wasn't his father, who had swallowed a load of grapeshot in the stomach. It wasn't him, either, that she had tried to kill. He was never ill and had never needed an herbal remedy; he also knew that she adored him. The first time he had come home late one evening—and certainly not for a good reason—she had made herself sick with worry.

Was it a deed prior to his birth? His father had married her for her beauty when she was hardly twenty years old. Had their wedding been preceded by an escapade allowing for some kind of crime?

No, not at all. Her crystal-clear past was known to him; he had heard it a hundred times, and accounts were altogether too consistent. So why, then, this terrible avowal? Why, surely, what! Why did he have to witness it?

Drunk with horror and despair, he returned home.

His mother immediately rushed up to kiss him:

"How late you are, dear child! And how pale! Could you be ill?"

"No," he replied, "I'm not ill. But the great heat has tired me, and I don't think I can eat. And you, mama, don't you feel a little unwell? You went out, I'm sure, to get a little fresh air? I think I saw you from far away, on the embankment."

"I did go out, but you couldn't have seen me on the embankment. *I went to confession*—something I believe you haven't done for quite a while, you naughty boy."

Jacques was surprised he didn't gasp and fall down thunderstruck (as always happened in the fine novels he read).

So it was true: she had been to confession! He hadn't fallen asleep in the church, then; the appalling catastrophe was no nightmare—as he had imagined in a moment of madness.

He didn't faint, but he grew much paler. His mother was frightened: "What is it, then, my little Jacques?" she asked. "You're not well, you're hiding something from your mother. You should have more trust that she loves you and only you . . . How you're staring! My sweet treasure . . . . But what's wrong? You're scaring me! . . ."

She took him tenderly in her arms.

"Listen to me, you big baby. I don't like to pry, you know, and I don't want to judge you. Don't say anything if you don't want to, but let me take care of you. Go to bed right away. Meanwhile, I'll make you a nice little meal, a light one, and I'll bring it to you myself, how about that? And if you have a fever tonight, I'll make you a cup of TEA . . ."

This time, Jacques collapsed on the floor.

"Finally!" she sighed, somewhat weary, and reached to ring for a servant.

Jacques had a severe *aneurysm*, and his mother had a lover who didn't want to be a stepfather.

This simple drama occurred three years ago in the neighborhood of Saint-German-des-Prés. The house that served as its theater now belongs to a demolitions contractor.

II. The Old Man of the House

Ah! How Madame Alexandre could pride herself on her virtue! Just think! For three years she had tolerated him, that old swindler—that old string of stewed beef disgracing her house. You can just imagine that if he hadn't been her father, she'd have long since slapped a return ticket on him: off to rot in the public infirmary!

But no! Unless one is descended from wild dogs, propriety simply must be observed, and the author of one's days provided for. Especially when you're in business.

"Oh! The family! Shame of shames! Some say God exists and that He is good! Surely the old goat will croak one of these days?"

Alas, the extreme frequency with which this filial monologue had occurred caused it to lose some of its freshness. Not a day passed that Madame Alexandre did not lament, in these terms, the cruelty of her fate.

But sometimes she grew tender—when she had to share the contents of her soul with young customers who would have understood the nobility of her complaints only imperfectly.

"Good, dear papa," she cooed, "If only you knew how loved he is! We love him wholeheartedly here. Business doesn't matter, you know! We might well have *come down a little*—had some hard luck, if you will—but the heart always speaks true. Memories of childhood, the wholesome joys of family; I feel restored to my proper place in my own eyes, I swear, when I see the honorable old man scurrying this way and that in the house, crowned by white hairs that call to mind our home in heaven." Etc., etc.

No doubt, professional carelessness allowed the hussy to operate, with equally good faith, by assuming either one pose or the other; the septuagenarian guest of Number 12, crowned by glory and disgrace in turn, rotted away at his daughter's side in the unchanging serenity of the evening of life—like a hospital rag on the bank of the sewer.

In the simplest of terms, the story of these two individuals has none of the qualities required for an epic poem.

The good-natured Ferdinand Bouton, informally known as "Papa Ferdinand" or the "*Old Man*," had belonged to the riffraff on the Rue de Flandre, where he formerly practiced some thirty trades—the least unmentionable of which had put his life at risk on several occasions.

Mademoiselle Léontine Bouton, who would one day become Madame Alexandre (and whose mother passed away shortly after giving birth to her), had been brought up by the worthy gentleman according to the principles of a most scrupulous lack of integrity.

Readied for field exercises from a tender age, at thirteen she assumed the distinguished position of a virginal oblate at the house of a Genevan millionaire esteemed for his virtue; this man called her his "angel of light" and perfected her ruination. Two years were all the debutante needed to finish off the Calvinist.

After that one, how many others there had been! Recommended above all to discreet gentlemen, she became something like an investment for many a *pater familias*; until she was eighteen, she walked in a nimbus of turpitude.

At that point, having come into her own by virtue of rubbing up against people *who meant business*, she dismissed her father; now that it yielded to idleness, his drunken, knavish frivolity outraged her sentiments.

And then fifteen years flowed by, during which the dissolute man gorged himself upon misfortune.

Unaccustomed to commerce and no longer commanding his old tricks, he resembled an old fly without the vigor to make its way to a pile of excrement—a creature in which even the spiders took no interest.

Léontine was luckier, and she flourished. Without rising to the highest echelons of Public Gallantry (whose command her incorrigibly boorish manners denied), she nevertheless was able to maneuver through subordinate offices with so much skill and such obliging ambidextrousness—she threaded her way, took position, settled in so firmly at the feast, and (never forgetting to fill her glass before the bottle stopped going 'round) was so *vicious* in the sight of God and men—that she managed to defy misfortune.

And so, misfortune took the form of her colorless, ghostly father.

Just as he was sinking forevermore into the most unsoundable abyss, the funny old man learned that his daughter—his Titine, now celebrated as Madame Alexandre—directed, with an imperious hand, a notorious enterprise where princes from the Far East came to offer their riches.

Verminous and covered with unclean rags—"with no radish in the cellar and nothing in the larder"—he happened by one fine day; fortune smiled on him so greatly that the haughty empress, although livid at his arrival, was obliged to welcome him with the most conspicuous displays of love.

Indeed, bad luck would have it that—at the very moment he forced his way past the guards and fell into her arms—she happened to be taking counsel with strict elders unable to disregard the Fourth Commandment of Divine Law. Indeed, one of them—moved by the pathetic scene deep within his very bowels—could not fail to pronounce a benediction predicting her eternal life.

Following so great a blow, Papa Ferdinand was impossible to shake loose—much less uproot. Under pain of provoking the indignation of honest folk and losing the profitable esteem of the mandarins, it was necessary to scrub off the dirt, clothe him, lodge him, and feed him every day.

Life, though sweet as honey until then, now was poisoned for Madame Alexandre. This father of hers was the princess's pea, the pickle her soul was caught in, and the timetable of her digestive tract; unlike Calypso, she took no comfort in Ulysses's return.

For all that, he was not cumbersome in the least. From the first day on, he was planted in the farthest part of the attic—its most inconvenient (and probably unhealthiest) corner. One hardly saw him. He faithfully observed instructions not to roam about the house when customers were there—and certainly never to set foot in the salon.

Nothing further was required to break with this strict law than the whim of a foreign amateur asking to see the Old Man about whom all these ladies spoke in whispers of fearful veneration—as if they were talking of the Man in the Iron Mask.

For circumstances such as these, he was given a scarlet leotard with decorative braids and a kind of Macedonian cap, which made him look like a Hungarian or a Pole facing adversity. Then, he received the title of count— Count Boutonski!—and he passed for a wreck decorated with glory, a ruin of the latest insurrection.

In turn, he cleaned the latrines, swept the stairs, and dried the basins and dishes—sometimes with the same cloth, Madame Alexandre remarked angrily. Finally, he did the shopping for the boarders whose confidence he enjoyed, and who tipped him handsomely.

In hours of leisure, the fortunate Old Man withdrew into his room and diligently read the works of Paul de Kock or the humanitarian elucubrations of Eugène Perspiration, as he called the author of *The Mysteries of Paris* and *The Wandering Jew* (the two loveliest books in the world).

Needless to say, the establishment went downhill during the war. Clients were in the country or on the ramparts, and the state of siege rendered the sidewalks impassable.

Madame Alexandre's exasperation reached a pitch. From morning to night, she never stopped breathing her rage at the Old Man; as she belched forth her curses without cease, he shriveled up more and more.

In her delirium, she went so far as to accuse him of sparking the international conflict with his little schemes. When the ransom of five billion francs was reached, she acted as if she had been despoiled herself and ranted that it amounted to as much money her business had lost—that one should line up all the old bastards who had brought on such misfortune and shoot them . . .

She grew positively rabid, and life became impossible.

It goes without saying that the Commune proved incapable of reinvigorating her shaky enterprise. For all that, customers were not wanting. Attendance never let up for a minute. One might have thought the establishment a church!

But what customers, Lord of the Heavens! Red drunkards, murderers, and vile roustabouts striped from head to foot, who ordered drinks with a revolver in hand and broke everything—and would have burned it down, too, if anyone had been bold enough to refuse them.

But this time, the landlady didn't make a scene. She was slowly dying of fear as she waited for help from above.

It was not long in coming. News suddenly came that troops from Versailles had entered Paris. Deliverance! All the same, a truly black hex cursed the poor creature.

It so happened that a barricade was erected at the end of the street. Now or never was the time to close the door, lock all the bolts, and pretend to be dead. Papa Ferdinand was forgotten entirely.

The barricade was taken at two o'clock in the afternoon as the fleeing federates abandoned the quarter. Soon, no one was left except for a solitary being—a slight old man whose steps echoed in the vast silence.

It was impossible not to recognize him. In his senility, he had left the house that morning, out of curiosity; then, stupidly, he ran like a criminal from the troops in red trousers.

The latter, on their guard, did not immediately pursue him, and they hesitated to shoot at a man of such advanced age. But they came running when they saw him stop at the door of Number 12.

"Out with the password and hands up!"

The Old Man, panting in terror, dove for the bell and started ringing.

"Titine, my Titine, it's me! Open up for your old father."

The shuttered window of the unseemly establishment opened right away. Madame Alexandre, drunk with *joy*, pointed her father out to the soldiers. She cried:

"Well, shoot him, goddammit! He was with the other ones. He's a dirty Communard—an arsonist who tried to set fire to the whole neighborhood."

Nothing more was required in those days of grace, and Papa Ferdinand, riddled with bullets, fell at the doorstep . . . .

Today, Madame Alexandre has retired from commerce and no longer lives at the exchange of which she was so long the glory. She collects thirty thousand francs per month from her investments, weighs nine hundred pounds, and sheds tears while reading the novels of Paul Bourget.

III. The Religion of Monsieur Pleur

> Generally speaking, the few people whom I have disliked
> in this world were flourishing people, of good repute.
> Whereas the knaves whom I have known, one and all, and
> by no means few, I think of with pleasure and kindness.
>
> THOMAS DE QUINCEY

The very sight of the old man engendered vermin. The dung heap of his soul extended so far into his hands and face one could not possibly imagine a more frightful contact. When he walked the streets, the slimiest gutters, shuddering at the reflection of his image, seemed to flow back to their source.

His fortune was reputed to be colossal, and worthy judges shed tears of ecstasy when they made their estimates; yet it was said to be hidden in maddening places, and no one could venture a solid guess about this nightmare's financial investments.

It was simply affirmed that, on various occasions, his cadaverous hand had been glimpsed in certain monetary schemes culminating in sublime disasters that a few frog-breeders thought he had arranged.

He was no Jew, however. When anyone treated him as an "old scoundrel," he had a gentle way of responding—"*May God repay you!*"—that made a tremor run down the spine of even the most cunning rogues.

The only matter that seemed certain was that this appalling mass of rags owned a house that brought him great revenue from one district or another that was famous for eccentricity. No one knew the details. Perhaps he owned several.

Legend held that he slept in a dark lair beneath a service staircase, between latrine pipes and the room of the concierge (whom his nearness had rendered idiotic).

His rent receipts were delivered for economy's sake, I was told, on scraps torn from printed matter that lodgers with connections resold to wily collectors.

The story also circulated—which quickly become notorious—of a fantastical soup regularly watered every Sunday evening; it was supposed to nourish him all week long. To avoid using any fuel, he ate it cold for six days in a row.

By Tuesday, of course, this alimentation had grown rotten. Then, with the reverent manners of a priest opening the tabernacle, he would take, from a small chest lodged in the wall (which must also have contained strange documents) a bottle of very old rum that likely had been fished out of some shipwreck.

He then poured some precious drops into a tiny glass and steeled himself in anticipation of savoring them after he had gobbled up his poultice. Once the operation was complete, he said:

"Now that you have eaten your soup, *there will be no* little nip of rum for you!"

And cruelly, he poured the precious liquid back into the bottle. This commendable ruse had always worked—for thirty or forty years.

No ghost ever seemed so bare of style and character. Because of his tattered clothes and, no doubt, some of his practices, he may well have resembled the most despised yids of Budapest or Amsterdam. For all that, the imagination of a Prometheus could not have discovered in him the slightest trace of antiquity.

The nickname "Shylock," bestowed by offenders of a lower order, was as outrageous as blasphemy, for this miser expressed nothing but dullness.

There was nothing terrible except his griminess and the stench he exuded of a knackered beast. But even that showed a dispiritingly modern quality. His filth did not assure him welcome in any abyss.

At least *in appearance*, he embodied nothing but the BOURGEOIS, the Mediocre—the "Killer of Swans," as Villiers put it—completely and definitively fulfilled; such as it must appear at the end of time, when Earthquakes emerge from their dens and corrupted souls are exposed to broad day!

Were it innocent to prostitute words, one would have to liken Monsieur Pleur to a horrible prophet, the Annunciator of God's Vomitations.

To the comfortable individuals his presence disgusted, he seemed to say:

"Don't you understand, my human brethren, that I am *translating* you for the Eternal—that my unclean carcass reflects you wondrously? When the truth shall be known, you will discover once and for all that I was your true country—so much so that, once come to vanish, the pestilence of your spirits will yearn for me. You will be nostalgic for my foul proximity: it made you seem to live, even though you were lower than the dead. Hypocritical bastards who hate in me the silent denunciation of your turpitude: the physical revulsion I inspire is the very measure of your minds' abominations. After all, what vermin devour me if not your own—swarming down to the depths of my heart?"

The queer man's gaze was especially intolerable to the elegant women he seemed to abhor. Sometimes he transfixed them with a beam paler than the phosphorescence of communal graves. A funereal and *viscous* wink stuck to their flesh like the spittle of a *vrukolak*—and they carried it off with them, screaming in fright.

"Isn't it true, sweetheart"—they seemed to hear—"that you will come to our assignation? I'll show you around my lovely grave, and you'll see the pretty jewelry of snails and black beetles I'll give you to accent the whiteness of your divine skin. I love you like a canker, and my kisses, I promise, have a higher price than any divorce. You too will stink one day, my pink mouse; you'll stink voluptuously by my side, and we'll be two pots underneath the stars . . ."

Then again, it would have been difficult—despite his hideous gaze—to determine a feature wholly characteristic of Monsieur Pleur.

Only his voice, perhaps—a voice of nasty mildness, which suggested an immodest sexton whispering disgraceful things.

For example, he had a way of pronouncing the word "money" that abolished the idea of metal and the value it represented. One heard something like *me-* or *mah-*, depending on the circumstances. Often, one heard nothing at all. The word fell into a faint.

That gave rise to a kind of abrupt modesty: a curtain falling all at once before the sanctuary, or the unexpected fear of seeming obscene while unbuttoning an idol.

Imagine, should it take your fancy, a fanatical sculptor. A bloodthirsty and sugary Pygmalion points out Galatea's perspective; all the while, he underhandedly makes you step backward into a trapdoor gaping to devour you.

It was so strong, this jealous passion for Money, that a few people had been fooled. They attributed horrid vices to this impenitent soul devoted to the cashbox and the vault. Though unjust, these suspicions were vouchsafed by some exegetes who were knowledgeable about the lives of others—ones who had caught him in mysterious exchanges with women and children on the street.

Sometimes, his form of worship found expression in such ecstatic circumlocutions—the slobbering erethism of his fervor softened his hardened gravedigger's face so much, and such improper sighs poured from his breast—that the modest urns in which he elected to drop the rare word may be excused for not feeling the hypochondriac majesty of *Idolatry* passing between them.

I will be exempted, I hope, from making known the exceptional circumstances that brought about friendly relations between this agreeable personage and myself.

I was young at the time—very young indeed—and easily given to enthusiasm. Monsieur Pleur took joy in soaking me with the same by revealing himself to me.

I believe I am the only person to have been admitted into his confidence. Let me add that his memory has greatly helped me to tolerate a destiny worse than a dog's life—and that today (the party in question being dead for quite some time) my conscience urges me to testify on behalf of this unrecognized man.

Some of my generation may recall his tragic end, which occurred during the last years of the Empire and prompted a little commotion.

To be sure, the actual murder—newspapers brought the details as far as the environs of the North Cape—was most banal; there's no arguing that the blackguards who committed it hardly deserved the celebrity they found.

The old man had simply been strangled where he nested—by bandits who had enjoyed no notoriety until then, and who avowed no motive other than robbery.

All the same, for a few months, circumstances relating to the victim's past (which were never clarified) exercised the vain sagacity of contemporaries.

It was determined that Monsieur Pleur *had not been what he seemed to be.*

In a word, the unlucky robbers—who, incidentally, managed to get caught with great ease—had been unable to locate the slightest treasure in the miser's den. And even though he died intestate and without natural heirs, the State also proved unable to fasten its claws on any sort of property.

It was found that the deceased had possessed absolutely nothing at all . . . except for an annuity from—and the usufruct of—an enormous fortune he had surrendered into the hands of a certain *Bishop.*

It is impossible to know what became of the considerable sums that must have passed his way in so many years of personally issuing receipts for legions of tenants.

No title, no stock, and nothing but nothing. Just the celebrated bottle of rum (which the cutthroats emptied).

Since this is barely a tale at all, I have the right not to offer a more dramatic conclusion. It bears repeating: I wish only to bear witness—in all likelihood, the only testimony that could face up to the wrathful shade of the deceased.

May I have leave, then, to sum up in a few lines the rather curious words spoken to me on various occasions by this solitary man, ordinarily so quiet.

I don't think I will ever feel so black a shudder as that day long ago, when we sat side by side on a bench in the Jardin des Plantes. He spoke to me as follows:

"My avarice scares you. Very well, little friend, I once knew a *prodigal* man—his kind is less rare than commonly believed; perhaps his story will make you wish to kiss my rags out of respect—should you be gifted enough to understand it.

"This prodigal individual was a maniac, of course. It's always easy to say so, and it relieves one of any deeper investigation. If you prefer, let us even call him a monomaniac.

"His fixed idea was *to throw* BREAD *into latrines*!

"To this end, he bankrupted himself at bakeries. One never met him but he was carrying a great loaf under his arm; skipping with joy, he was off to cast it into the public toilets.

"He lived only to perform this deed. One must believe it gave him the fiercest pleasure. His joy positively became madness when opportunity arose to present the spectacle to poor devils dying of hunger.

"He had thirty thousand francs in income, the party in question, yet he complained how expensive bread was.

"Consider well this tale; though true, it sounds like a parable."

I did not conceive the desire to kiss the rags of Monsieur Pleur, but the sense of his narrative was clear enough to me all the same: I thought that I heard, galloping beneath me, the cavalry of the Pit.

The last time I met this Plato of avarice, he said:

"Do you know that Money is God and that this is the reason men seek it with such zeal? No, it's not like that? You're too young for it to have dawned upon you. You would surely take me for some kind of madman if I told you that It is infinitely good, infinitely perfect—this sovereign Lord of all things—and that nothing happens in this world without Its command or Its permission; that, in consequence, we are created solely to know It, to adore and serve It—that we may earn, by this means, Life Eternal.

"You would revile me were I to speak of the mystery of Its *Incarnation*. No matter! Know that not a day passes but I pray for Its Kingdom to arrive and for Its Name to be sanctified.

"I also ask that Money, my Redeemer, deliver me from all evil, from all sin, from the snares of the Devil, and from the spirit of fornication. I entreat It for Its Idleness as much as for Its Joys and Its Glory.

"One day you will understand, my boy, how this God has debased Himself for us. Remember the maniac I spoke of! And behold to what works human malice has condemned Him!

"For my part, I have not so much as dared touch It for thirty years!... Yes, young man, for thirty years I have not dared put my dirty paws on a fifty-cent coin! When my lodgers pay me, I put their money in a precious vessel, made of olive wood, which once touched the Tomb of Christ; I do not keep it for even a single day.

"I am, if you would know, a *penitent of Money*.

"With inexpressible consolation, I endure, for Its sake, to be scorned by men, even to strike terror in the hearts of beasts, and to be crucified every day of my life by the most wretched poverty..."

I had looked deeply enough into the mysterious existence of this extraordinary individual to see he was speaking a wholly symbolic language. All the same, I confess that Scripture, translated so harshly, frightened me a bit.

All of a sudden, he rose up and lifted his arms. I can still see him, like a double gallows from which the rotted scraps of an ancient victim were hanging.

"People often say," he cried out, "that I am an appalling miser. Well, then! One day, you will tell that I found a hiding-place—infinitely secure—which no miser before me ever knew:

I buried my Money in the Bosom of the Poor! . . .

"You will make it known, my child, the day that Scorn and Pain have made you great enough to seek out the supreme honor of being misunderstood."

Monsieur Pleur fed about two hundred families. Among them, one would have sought in vain a single party who did not consider him a lowlife. That's how clever he was!

But today, heavenly justice! Where teems the pallid multitude of the destitute assisted by the episcopal agent of this Penitent?

IV. The Parlor of Tarantulas

In 1869, during my radiant youth, I met the poet at the residence of Barbey d'Aurevilly. His wild hair and ranting mouth captured my interest right away.

He was shaggy and white, and bore a head that seemed to defy shearing in perpetuity. Even though he was scarcely forty years old, his thick fleece the color of snow blowing in the wind lent him, from far away, the likeness of an exultant Saturn or a Jupiter-of-the-Dynamite prematurely aged by unbelievable abuses in houses of abandon.

His small face of smashed bricks staring out from under the snowflakes boiled more and baked redder each time one looked at it.

His chronic irritation astounded even him:

"I am the *Parlor of Tarantulas*!" he cried in a voice destined for the straitjacket, making the little factory women hasten their steps on the street.

Poor d'Aurevilly, who would one day succumb to the web of the black spider of Languedocian occultism, never failed to stoke the rage of this volcanic poetaster—he was altogether incapable of resigning himself to any attention, however distinguished in kind, that did not grant him first place (or, better yet, exclusive consideration).

Damascène Chabrol had been a physician—or, rather, he still was one, for one can affirm that medicine *shapes character* just as much as does the Priesthood. But he no longer needed to earn any sort of living and had long sickened of purgating merchants and analyzing their secretions. Consequently, he had eliminated his clientele—to avoid a stronger word he usually employed—and generously devoted himself to the most resolute cultivation of verse.

At the time, I believed he was not entirely unfit to strike the lyre, and, if I remember correctly, several literary authorities shared the opinion.

God knows what I might think today! Alas, life is so short—and its span so uncertain—that verily I should fear to wear out the precious thread of existence by excavating, from under dust accumulated over twenty-five years, the two or three forgotten collections that he published.

I should add, even while conceding the genius of the deceased, that no poem from his hand could equal the matchless night we spent together in his quarters, Rue de Fleurus, four days before his terrible death. It was not—I implore you to believe me—a night spent in love.

Three savage passions dwelt within him: little ladies, grand verses, and desire for renown.

Since each of these sentiments undeniably possessed the quality of a paroxysm, I never quite understood how they could coexist in one person—and especially the first with the other two.

The man's temper was deadly, like that of a possessed patriarch kneeling at the venerable, soiled rags of the late Sainte-Beuve. At least the latter had had nothing patriarchal about him—it was an act of generosity, on the part of the Second Empire, that the violence of his sudden fantasies should have been given the means to dissipate at nearby garrisons or in the shrubbery of the Luxembourg Gardens without making a regrettable scene.

The intervals that punctuated these crises—as he waited for the buck in him to revive—were devoted to recopying his works, rushing into the whirlwind of inspired breaths like a petrel in a hurricane.

Thereupon emerged a swarm of visions, half-visions, flashes of heat, total eclipses, blasphemies indicting the unresponding firmament, and invocations familiarly *whispered* into the ear of all the demons—until, finally, he was left sprawling on his carpet, grinding his teeth and twisting in epileptic convulsions.

It was difficult to gain entry to his quarters. He always seemed afraid that something subtle, a matter infinitely rare and precious, would escape through the open door, descend the stairs, pass the gloomy concierge, and disgrace itself in the infinite shame of the dogs on the street . . .

Consequently, he would not open up when one knocked. Or if he did, he barely opened, holding the door a millimeter from the frame while his free hand performed great, silent gestures—as if, within his dwelling, a sublime death were occurring and, to assure the balance of the universe, it was necessary that the last gasp pass undisturbed.

If the visitor was not scared off by the lonesome man's flaming eyes and wished to proceed despite the strange welcome, it was impossible to enter quickly enough; the door immediately slammed shut in a gust of wind, like a mousetrap snapping on a shrew. I can vouchsafe that few mortals ever mustered the necessary boldness.

The forbidding Damascène would hunch over and rub his hands; his palms pressed together just under his chin and pointed downward, expressing the joy of a cannibal sure of his prey.

Then his fanfare of recriminations would explode for the course of an hour. He became a torrent of complaints; one heard its muffled roar and mounting murmur when it started far away, up in blue mountains; then, growing clearer and clearer, the hoarse bellowing would spread in the manner of a giant sheet, until finally, it thundered in an immense fracas of dislocation and collapse as the clamor poured together.

They weighed greatly upon his heart, indeed! I imagine nothing short of death would have kept him from vociferating, *even as he slept*, against publishers, journals, the Academy, members of the Comédie Française, and, in general, the entire mass of humanity that persisted in denying him his due.

Perhaps he was right. Again, I affirm that I know nothing of it and also wish to know nothing. I am sufficiently intoxicated by indignation of my own that I have no need to inebriate myself with that of others.

I am getting to the poem of that night—one notable among so many others, which was not spent in love.

In entirely unwonted fashion, Damascène Chabrol had extended a written invitation to come to his house—not for dinner (which would have been healthy and, consequently, banal in the extreme), but to listen to him read one of his dramas (a prospect that struck me as dangerous and altogether terrifying).

His missive—which, incidentally, was more threatening than fraternal—left no doubt as to the seriousness of the matter. He positively demanded that I be punctual and declared that justice would have it so.

The form of the invitation did not repulse me. Right away, my curiosity was keenly roused, and I found that *justice* and my own wishes agreed. I was prompt; behold, without further ado, what then occurred.

At the first knock, the door opened. I was conducted inside according to the aforementioned rite.

Damascène was calmer than I had dared expect. Indeed, he was tremendously calm—and I could not refrain from comparing him to a professional thief or hangman on the verge of exercising his functions. I was worlds away from suspecting how precise the analogy was.

Two glasses of grog had been prepared; on the table lay the imposing manuscript, opened wide before one of the two chairs.

Fortunately, the weather was mild. Had it been too cold or too hot, I could very easily have died that night; the most elaborate precautions had been taken that I should appreciate the absolute uselessness of attempting to interrupt, however briefly or legitimate the occasion.

"*The Daughter of Jephthah! A Biblical Drama in Five Acts,*" he began, fixing his implacable gaze upon me.

At first, the exercise did not displease me. The reader had a bizarre, gastralgic voice, which rose effortlessly from profound basses up to the sharpest, childlike tones. He *spoke* like this and truly played his drama, performing gestures that included falling to his knees in prayer when events so required. The curious spectacle amused me for an hour—that is, for as long as the first act. The unconscionable monster went so far as to take whole scenes from the top when he feared I might not have felt all their beauty; no words of admiring protest could restrain him.

In act 2—when his mimicry had lost the charm of the unexpected—I dared truly listen.

It was deplorable. Just imagine: the dustiest, filthiest, most impudent and fetid clichés. A terrible amalgamation of Racine, the venerable Gagne, and de Désaugiers. It called to mind an interminable discourse on agriculture and social economy declaimed by his Judge . . .

Near the end of act 3, I feigned a sudden need of the most vulgar kind—hoping, in this way, to make it to the stairs. The pestilential man accompanied me . . .

I had to swallow it whole, and it took until midnight. I had been *sacrificed* almost as much as the selfsame daughter of Israel's Liberator.

But what became of me when—making a dash for my hat—Damascène spoke the following words, seemingly culled from the Book of Revelation:

"Oh, no! Don't be in a rush, *we haven't read anything yet*. I won't let you go until you've heard my sonnets."

A man ignorant of the French tongue might have thought he was offering me a cup of chocolate. Then he announced *fifteen hundred sonnets*—more than twenty thousand lines!—and his voice, far from having tired from its previous exertions, was now clearer, fresher, more balanced, and abler, it seemed, to play the trombone until the fall of the heavens (which, unfortunately, failed to occur).

What to do? He had shown me that the only way out was over the dead body of a madman; at the time (as is still the case today), I did not practice the venial custom of staining my hands in blood.

I sat down again, suppressing a groan of despair.

Five minutes later, I was sleeping soundly. The ringing of an alpine cowbell, vigorously shaken next to my ear, woke me up.

"Ah! Ah! You're sleeping, I believe," my executioner said to me.

"My God!" I replied, "I'm just resting my eyes . . . But I confess I am a little bit tired."

"Very well, I know how it is."

At that, he opened a drawer, pulled out a revolver that seemed to defy ordinary dimensions, loaded it carefully, and placed it on the table—without lifting his hand from the butt. Raising the manuscript in his left hand, he simply added:

"I'll continue! . . ."

The torture lasted until sunrise. At that moment, he rose mechanically, closed his accordion, and informed me that he was off to catch a train.

"I'm going to see Papa," he explained.

A few hours later, having arrived in Orleans, he slapped about his seventy-five-year-old father. And immediately after, he threw himself down a well. He was dragged up, raving mad, and locked in the shed where, the following day, he died in a complete frenzy.

To my great surprise, I inherited a considerable part of his fortune. It is with his money—if you must know—that I had such a good time from the age of twenty-five to thirty, as everyone knows.

V. Draft for a Funeral Oration

Hardly anyone knows he just died. When the great mass of those who consider themselves still to number among the living learns of his death, the papers will print vividly clichéd laments about the great writer "we have so painfully lost" (after having scorned him so basely in his lifetime).

Such grief, which the profession will intone in a single voice, will be gathered in spades, like cemetery dirt, by our chronicles' gravediggers. It will extend as far as the feet of "his friend during the final hours"—an unsavory, lupine novelist in need of just such advertising, who *hijacked* his dying moments and made his death even more bitter.

Let us content ourselves simply to call him "Lazarus," this man deceased in barest indigence—who rightfully should have worn one of the greatest crowns of nobility in the whole of the Occident.

"I belong," he had declared, "to the race of Beings who dignify other men."

For this reason, he would never hear of "a homeland other than exile"—and as a result, life was prodigiously awful for this poor, sublime devil.

Later, when the false flames of sweltering, posthumous admiration are extinguished—a little or much later—I will speak of his death; its sadness and horror, so carefully concealed, can hardly be exceeded.

For I have a great deal to share—I assure you—and dark matter abounds.

But today, that is not my intention. I would simply like, apropos of this Lazarus—whom everyone has the right to consider imaginary—to verify, by the light of a piteous torch, the most decisive of adages concerning aristocracy (which the Revolution believes it has killed off).

"Each man augments his race." Thus did the philosopher Blanc de Saint-Bonnet bring together—as if forging a blade of bronze—the wisdom of the ages.

That is to say: on the outermost point of the last branch of a great tree elected by lightning, there always hangs a fruit—delectable or horrifying—which collects a precious essence before it vanishes forever.

When the matter involves glorious sap, as in the case of our Lazarus, the tender vessel bearing all the weight does not sustain only the splendors and miseries, the divine joys and profound griefs, the humiliations and triumphs that all his ancestors have accumulated. In addition, he must carry the whole Dream, and do so across a vast, never-ending desert—"from the womb to the sepulcher"—without a single soul to aid or console him.

He must suffer the miraculous and fearsome inheritance of a breast that heaves with all the sighs of generations—whose very name lies in the death throes . . .

Nor is that all, O, my God! Behold the abyss of woe.

The destiny of Lazarus was so extraordinary that his own life seemed to distill the entire history of the haughty Race he supremely incarnated.

Perhaps a kind of analogy will facilitate comprehension.

Do you remember those epitomized chronicles that pedagogues insatiate of curses inflicted on our childhood years? Each age is condemned to draw its breath from just four narrow pages—out of asphyxiating opuscules where the most remote and unrelated events pile on top of each other and press together like salted meats in the barrels of a merchant.

Charlemagne pushes up against Merovech; the first Valois are glued to the Valois of Orleans or to the Valois of Angouleme; Henry III is crushed alongside Charles the Wise; Francis I is flattened on top of Louis the Fat;

Ravaillac murders Jean Sans Peur; evidently, Louis XIV signs the Revocation of the Edict of Nantes at Varennes, and so on. All perspective goes missing, and the chaos cannot be untangled.

Lazarus—the last of his line with nothing left before him except the mounting Boorishness of the fin-de-siècle—was, after a fashion, a dreadful digest of this kind.

Incapable of adjusting to modern life, which filled him with disgust, he dwelt at the bottom of his own heart—like a dragon from before the Flood in its lair, disconsolately raging that his kind has been extinguished.

Truly, he bore within him the souls of all the great men of his House, and the list was long. He would confabulate with their shades. Nor did he disrespectfully seek to separate them; on the contrary, he was happy that he no longer knew what, in due justice, belonged to each one of them.

Moreover, he was one of those rare adepts who refuse death and convince themselves that survival is an act of will—that it is incomparably easier to eternalize oneself than to make a simple end.

Accordingly, he held that death, which so many dunces chatter on about, is nothing but imposture—an untenable contrivance concocted by florists and the manufacturers of tombstones.

For personal use, he had even devised a fantasy—a Hegelian one, alas!—on the theme; here, he meant to establish that beings and things cannot endure before the Infinite in a manner other than the form our consciousness pleases to grant them.

And so he lived in the midst of a glorious assembly whose resurrection he had long since performed—one that easily brought together warriors and magistrates separated by the expanse of centuries, whose personalities vanished for him in the magnificent throng of individuals of his own blood.

This man's infernal existence is well enough known. It has become the stuff of marvelous legend, even though its bizarre circumstances—which some parties' malicious imaginings have embroidered—were, in actual fact, much rarer than is commonly supposed.

His notoriously dark wit was nothing, all things considered, but the turmoil of his poor soul. As such, it was rather tragic.

I have stated that his life was shaped to fit the very History of his Race, and that herein lay the principle of suffering without name. But how can one make such matters understood?

This history that occupies the center of the Universal History—which one learns so poorly in school—was absolutely living and present within him. It burned and devoured like a raging flame for which he had provided the final tinder.

In his unremitting agonies, the slightest of gestures immediately recaptured the ancient *res gestae* of his whole quasi-royal Line (which then died, in the ventricles of his heart, with its boots on).

Very few mortals understood him—and what could they do for such a monumental wretch? He was a god himself, and the god Moloch had refused the continued existence of any aristocracy; a holocaust was in order.

He had been given literary genius in addition to everything else. It was the kindling of his torments.

How glorious his debuts had been! Twenty years old, dazzling men and women. Fanfares burst forth from every doorstep. Here was something new in the world—something altogether unheard-of, which everyone would surely venerate, for it offered the reflection, the faithful intaglio, of ancient Idols.

What did it matter he was poor? Was that not a further distinction? He held a beggar's sack filled with fruits like stars, gathered with both hands in the bright forest; nor could there be any doubt in Mankind.

But one day, it dawned on him that the people—grown sick of bread—clamored loudly for potatoes; it wanted the soles of its feet rubbed with the fat from the small intestines of Princes of Light. Thus began an agony that lasted for thirty years.

Sufficiently great numbers have borne witness that there is no need to tell it now. Courage fails me, moreover. As stated above, I reserve for myself only the final and supreme word, one that remains unknown—quite profoundly unknown, I assure you—and which I mean to reveal unsparingly.

On that day, the color of a certain *pontiff's* brow will be made plain.

VI. The Prisoners of Longjumeau

Yesterday, the *Postillon de Longjumeau* announced the appalling end of the Fourmis. This rag, rightly commended for its abundantly informative reports, lost itself in conjecture about the mysterious reasons for the despair that has plunged the couple—thought to be happily married—into suicide.

Joined at a very young age and still enjoying their honeymoon twenty years later, they never left the town for a *single* day.

The foresight of the authors of their days had relieved them of the monetary worries that can poison conjugal life; they were amply provided for (even if this runs counter to what is necessary to enliven a legitimate union and hardly fulfills the need for amorous vicissitude that ordinarily governs human whims); and they incarnated the miracle of perpetual affection in the eyes of the world.

One fine evening in May (the day after the fall of Monsieur Thiers), the great railroad line conducted them and their relations—who went along to see them set up a home—to the delightful property that was to harbor their joy.

With emotion, those residents of Longjumeau who were pure of heart watched the handsome couple pass by; without a moment's hesitation, the town veterinarian compared them to Paul and Virginie.

On that day they were truly well, looking just like the pale children of a *grand seigneur*.

The foremost solicitor of the district, Master Piécu, had procured for them a verdant nest the dead themselves would have envied, just where the town began. Indeed, one must grant that the garden recalled an abandoned cemetery. Evidently, its appearance did not displease them, for they made no changes and let the plants grow freely.

To employ one of Master Piécu's profoundly original turns of phrase, "they lived *in the clouds.*" The couple hardly saw anyone—and not out of malice or disdain, but simply because it never occurred to them.

What is more, they would have had to disentangle themselves for a few hours, or even minutes, and interrupt their raptures. Goodness me! Life is short, and the extraordinary pair didn't have the heart to do so.

One of the greatest men of the Middle Ages, Master Johannes Tauler, tells of a recluse, from whom an importunate visitor once demanded an item he kept in his cell. The monk went about entering his quarters to retrieve the object. But in so doing, he forgot what it was: the images of external reality did not stick in his mind. And so he came back out and asked the visitor to tell him again what he wanted. The latter repeated his request. The monk went back in—but before laying hold of said object, he had forgotten what it was. After several attempts, he was obliged to tell the bothersome individual: "Go in and look yourself for what you need; *I cannot keep your image within me* long enough to do as you ask."

Monsieur and Madame Fourmi often reminded me of this monk. They would have given gladly anything requested of them—had they proved able to remember what it was for even a moment.

Their distraction was notorious; people talked about it as far away as Corbeil. All the same, they did not appear to suffer for it, and so the "dreadful" resolution that put an end to their generally envied existence seems inexplicable.

An old letter from the unlucky Fourmi, whom I knew before he married, has enabled me to reconstruct, by way of induction, his pitiful story in its entirety.

Here is the letter. Perhaps it will be clear that my friend was neither a madman nor an imbecile.

. . . For the tenth or twentieth time, dear friend, it seems we are not keeping our word with you, outrageously. However great your patience, you must be tired of inviting us. The truth is that this last time, just as on the preceding occasions, we—my wife and I—have no excuse at all. We wrote that you could count on us, and we had absolutely nothing to do. All the same, we missed the train, as always.

For *fifteen years* we have missed all the trains and public cars, *no matter what we do.* It's infinitely idiotic, it's abominably ridiculous, but I'm starting to think that this ill is without remedy. It's a comical fate, and we are its victims. Nothing helps. We have even risen at three in the morning and spent the night without sleeping so as not to miss the train at eight o'clock, for example. Well, my dear man, the chimney caught fire at the last minute, I got a sprain halfway there, Juliette's dress tore on some bush, we fell asleep on the couch in the waiting room, and neither the train's arrival nor the attendant's shouting got us up in time, etc., etc. This last occasion, I forgot my wallet.

Anyway, I repeat, this has lasted for fifteen years, and I feel that the principle of our death rests here. For the same reason, as you know, I've made a mess of everything, I'm on bad terms with everyone, I'm considered an egotistical monster, and my poor Juliette is naturally suffocated by the same opprobrium. Since we arrived in this accursed place, I've missed seventy-four funerals, twelve marriages, thirty baptisms, and a thousand vitally important calls or appointments. I let my mother-in-law pass away without ever seeing her again—even though she was ill for about a year; that made us lose three-quarters of her estate: in a rage, she added a codicil snatching most of it away from us the night before she died.

There would be no end if I sought to list the blunders and misadventures caused by the unbelievable fact that we have never been able to get away from Longjumeau. In sum, *we are prisoners,* henceforth deprived of all hope—and we can see the time coming when being galley-slaves will cease to be tolerable . . .

I omit the rest—my sad friend confided things too intimate for publication. But I give my word of honor that he was not a coarse man, that he deserved the adoration of his wife, and that these two beings merited better than to end in the stupid and unsavory manner they did.

Certain details that I ask to keep for myself make me think that the unfortunate couple really was the victim of a shadowy plot hatched by the Enemy of mankind. He conducted them—by the hand of a solicitor who was clearly infernal—to that baleful corner of Longjumeau, from where no power could tear them away.

I truly believe they *could* not escape—that surrounding their dwelling stood a cordon of invisible *troops* carefully selected to keep watch, and no effort could possibly have prevailed against these forces.

The sign of diabolical influence, for me, was the fact that the Fourmis were consumed by a passion for travel. These captives were migratory by nature. Before they wed, they had yearned to tour the globe. When they were still just engaged, they had been sighted at Choisy-le-Roi, Meudon, Clamart, and Montretout. One day, they had made it as far as Saint-Germain.

In Longjumeau—which seemed like an island in Oceania to them—their hunger for bold journeys of exploration, for adventures on land and sea, had only increased.

Their house was filled with globes and planispheres; they had English atlases and German ones, too. They even owned a map of the Moon published at Gotha by a pedant named Justus Perthes.

When they were not making love, they would read the stories of famous navigators together; these works filled their library exclusively, and there was not a single travel journal, guide to world tours, or geographical bulletin to which they did not subscribe. Schedules of railroads and brochures from maritime agencies rained in without cease.

No one will believe it, but their bags were always packed. They were always just ready to depart—to undertake an interminable voyage to the most remote lands, wherever was most dangerous and least explored.

I received at least forty dispatches announcing their imminent departure for Borneo, Tierra del Fuego, New Zealand, or Greenland.

Several times, they had even been a hair's breadth away from actually leaving. But they didn't leave after all—they never did, because they were neither able nor permitted to leave. Atoms and molecules united to drag them backward.

But one day, ten years ago, they thought they had escaped for good. Against all hope, they managed to board a first-class carriage that would convey them to Versailles. Deliverance! There, no doubt, the magic circle would be broken.

The train started, but they didn't move. Naturally, they had landed in a car destined to remain at the station. They had to start all over again.

The only voyage they could not possibly miss, evidently, was the one they have just undertaken, alas! Their character, which is well known, prompts me to believe they readied themselves only in trembling.

VII. A Lousy Idea

There were four of them, and I knew them only too well. If it's all the same to you, we'll call them Theodore, Theodule, Theophile, and Theophrastus.

They were not brothers, but they lived together and never left each other's company for a minute. You couldn't see one of them without the other three showing up.

Of course, the chief of the squad was Theophrastus, the last to be named and the man of *Characters*. I think he deserved to command his companions, for he knew how to command himself.

He had the ways of a cut-and-dried Puritan: harnessed with his certainties, he was meticulous and probing. Outwardly, he displayed both the features of a badger and those of an assessor at a pawnshop in some poor neighborhood.

When one greeted him, it always seemed he was receiving a pledge—and his reply resembled a professional estimate.

On the inside, he had the stable soul of an unyielding mule—the kind they raise, with due attention, in England or in the city of Calvin, for the purpose of transporting whitewashed coffins.

For all that, he didn't want to be considered a Protestant. He declared he was Catholic to the bone and conspicuously left his heart to dry on the stakes that hold up the Vine of the Elect.

His concern was to be *chaste*, and certainly to appear so. Chaste as a nail, like pruning shears, like a kipper! His acolytes declared him imperishable and unpluckable—no less auroral and lactescent than the bright robes of angels.

Dare I say it? He viewed women as if they were excrement, and the height of madness would have been to incite him to bawdiness. In a general manner, he disapproved of any contact between the sexes, and any discourse evoking love struck him as a personal affront.

He was so chaste he would have condemned the dress of the Zouaves.

Such, in large traits was the physiognomy of this chieftain.

May it be permitted to sketch the others.

Theodore was the lion of the group. He was its pride and ornament, and whenever it was a matter of diplomacy or persuasion, he stepped forward (since Theophrastus lacked eloquence).

Although it is true that on such occasions Theodore would drink in order to roar better, he acquitted himself to general satisfaction.

He was a little Gascon lion—without a mane, unfortunately—who boasted of belonging to the celebrated family (more or less extinct today) of the Theodores of Saint-Antonin and Lexos, who once graced the banks of the Aveyron.

It would be unwell to ignore that his arms—the proud and noble arms of his ancestors—had been sculpted on the porch or at some other place of the Cathedral of Albi or Carcassonne. Travel was too expensive to pursue verification—but also unnecessary, for the gentleman had given his word of honor.

These arms, attentively copied onto paper of vegetable matter in the Bibliothèque Nationale, were not shown to me, but the motto—*That way, dammit!*—always struck me as both simple and magnificent.

In a word, this Theodore fascinated and dazzled his friends— whose ancestors, alas, had been refractory peasants. Still, he could not serve as their corporal inasmuch as glory must needs yield to wisdom. The dull but immaculate Theophrastus had bound them together so that the storms of life could not rend them asunder. He held them secure every day, imparting virtue and teaching them how to live and think; and so the hotheaded Achilles nobly agreed to obey the oracles of this Nestor.

Theodule and Theophile can be dealt with in a few words. The former had nothing remarkable about him, apart from the apparent hardiness of a docile and unwitting bull; one could have put him to work in a cemetery. He was happy to march when goaded, and he required almost no light.

The latter, in contrast, marched out of fear. He did not consider the band particularly witty or terribly amusing; still, having let himself be roped in by Theophrastus, he dared not even think of desertion and trembled lest he displease the imposing man.

He was very young—almost a child. He deserved better, I believe, for it seems he didn't lack sensitivity or intelligence.

Now behold the wretched idea—the imbecilic wreck of an idea pulled by these four individuals in a team. If anyone can find a lousier one, I shall be much obliged to learn of the same.

They imagined bringing to life the mysterious confederacy from *History of the Thirteen* that Balzac once dreamed up. It was *pagan* dream, if ever there was one. *Eadem velle, eadem nolle*, said Sallust—one of the most atrocious scoundrels of antiquity.

To have a single soul and a single brain divided among four epidermises—that is, at the end of the day, to renounce their personalities and become a number, a quantity, a package, fractions of a collective being. What a brilliant notion!

But the wine of Balzac proved too heady for these poor brains; once it had intoxicated them, the state seemed divine, and they bound themselves together by oath.

Did you read that? *By oath.* On what gospel, on what altar, on what relics did they swear? They did not tell me, unfortunately, for I should have liked to know. All I have been able to discover or surmise is that, by formulas of execration and having invoked all the pits to bear witness, they devoted themselves to the absurd existence of never harboring a thought that was not the thought of the group, never to love or hate anything that was not loved or hated in common, never to keep the slightest secret, to read all letters aloud, and to live together in perpetuity without separating for a single day.

Naturally, Theophrastus must have instigated the solemn act. The others could not have been that far gone.

Because the four of them all worked in the same ministerial office, it was possible to realize the essential part of the program. They shared the same quarters, the same table, the same clothes, the same creditors, the same promenades, the same readings, and the same defiance (or horror) of all that did not belong to their quadrille. And so they shared the same errors concerning people and things.

In order to be wholly among themselves, they vilely *dropped* old friends and benefactors—among them, an altogether great artist whose interest they had had the incredible good fortune of receiving for a moment, a man who had sought to advise them against their tendency to walk on all fours, like swine . . .

Years passed in this manner—and the best years of life, too. The eldest, Theophrastus, was hardly thirty when the association started. They almost achieved celebrity: ridicule grew so quickly wherever they trod that they were obliged to change neighborhoods several times.

People were touched when they saw these four sad men pass by—these bondsmen of Folly, all dressed in the same way and walking in a single gait; they seemed to be dragging their souls on the Earth, supervised by suspicious officers.

Naturally, it had to end dramatically. One day, the hot-blooded Theodore fell in love.

They entertained as few relationships as possible—but all the same, some did exist. A young girl unloved by God thought it well to marry a gentleman whose coat of arms adorned—there could be no doubt—either the Cathedral of Albi or the Cathedral of Carcassonne.

Needless to say, I won't recount the infinitely complicated story of this marriage, which modified—most completely and most profoundly—the mechanical existence of our heroes.

From the first fits of such illness, Theodore remained loyal to the program and opened his heart to his three friends; their stupefaction went beyond measure. First, Theophrastus breathed unbounded indignation and poured, in atrocious words, the blackest venom on all women without exception.

It almost came to blows, and the Holy Vehm was inches away from dissolving.

Theodule liquefied in pain, whereas Theophile—secretly starved for independence and harboring wishes that a revolution might occur (but not daring to voice as much)—guarded a dreary silence.

All the same, everything calmed down, and an artificial balance was restored. Each stone, raised for an instant, ponderously fell back into place. Theophrastus, the fearsome pawn, reflected that, all in all, his herd would increase by a unit, and so he finally embraced the hope of broader dominion.

The inseparable companions went as a single body to ask, on behalf of Theodore, for the hand of the unfortunate girl who failed see the abyss where her blind desire to marry the scion of a valorous knight had plunged her.

Hell began the very first day. It had been agreed that communal life would continue. Although it is true the newlyweds managed to be left alone during the night, it was still required that everyone rise at a certain hour—that no misstep occur when observing the most monastic of regulations.

Each morning, Theodore had to account fully for events in the darkness of the conjugal chamber. The poor woman soon discovered, to her horror, that she had married *four* men.

The most dreadful future unfolded before her eyes on the morning that followed her sorrowful nuptials. She recognized the dreadful folly of the upstart whose wife she had become and her humiliating state of slavery to a confederacy of dunces.

Her letters—her private possessions—were unsealed by the odious Theophrastus and read aloud before the three others, in her presence. The bison paraded his droppings and impure slobber on the confidences of women, mothers, and girls.

With her husband's consent, the tyranny of the loathsome pedant extended to her grooming, attire, diet, words, gazes, and slightest gestures.

Smothered, trampled underfoot, wilted, and despairing, she lapsed into deep silence and began to envy, with all her heart, those fortunate enough to travel in a coffin unattended by any mourners.

At first, the quadrille shut her in and double-locked the door when they went to the office (where the administration would not have permitted her presence).

Serious complications forced them to abandon such rigor. Then, she was free—at least, she must have thought she was free—to come and go for about eight hours a day.

She did not know that the concierge, receiving abundant emolument, was taking note of her exits and entries—and that spies scattered in neighboring streets carefully watched everything that she did.

And so, the prisoner took advantage of the illusion of freedom to intoxicate herself with an air different from that of the vile cloister, which she dared not breathe.

She went to see relatives and old friends; she strolled on the boulevard and along the river. In exchange, she was punished with scenes of diabolical violence and made more miserable still: Theodore, in addition to his other charming qualities, was as jealous as a Bluebeard of Kabylia.

It was too much. Then there occurred what naturally—*inevitably*—must occur under such a regime.

Madame Theodore listened, without displeasure, to the words of a stranger, who seemed a man of genius compared to those idiots. She thought him as handsome as a god because he did not resemble them and

infinitely generous because he spoke to her kindly. In a transport of unspeakable joy, she became his mistress on the spot.

What happened next was reported a few days ago in the papers.

I understand the same night she fell, when the four men gathered, the
Demon appeared to them.

VIII. Two Ghosts

Little was as distressing as the collapse of this friendship.

Mademoiselle Cleopatra du Tesson des Mirabelles de Saint-Pothin-sur-le-Gland and Miss Penelope Elfrida Magpie had cherished each other for thirty winters. They even wound up looking like each other.

The former belonged to the equine race of those unpardoning blue-stockings who cannot be bought—and whom no burnt offering can appease.

She had written twenty volumes of sociology and history, crushing as many publishers beneath her. There were not enough bookstands on the river to collect her tomes, which newspapers in their death throes offered as a premium to subscribers; this not-quite-invaluable packing material suitably rewarded the efforts of young pupils when schools distributed their prizes.

The daughter of a rugged translator of Homer—whose passing she alone mourned—and an appalling woman tanned by many solstices who was reputed an erstwhile spy, this Corinne of the sarcophaguses remained inconsolable for not having married, once upon a time, a famous man she thought had loved her.

Having been beautiful in olden times according to a few paleographers, with a shudder she had resigned herself to planting the Tree of Liberty amidst her own ruins.

Always dressed in black, *down to her very fingertips*, and her hair in a crow's nest, the rare slices of herself that a propriety altogether Britannic permitted her to expose were sticky with a thick layer of grime, and its first alluvial deposits surely went back to the July Revolution.

Her face resembled a fried potato rolled in scraped cheese. Her hands made one think she had "exhumed her great-grandmother," as a Scandinavian proverb puts it.

Finally, her whole person exuded the odor of a landing in a furnished hotel of the twentieth order—on the seventh floor.

All the same, she was greatly admired by a flock of young Englishwomen whose independent means were assured by raising livestock or the international traffic of prized Negroes who whiten with age.

They came from various points of the United Kingdom to Mademoiselle Tesson's to learn literature and the high manners of the *grand siècle*— which she was the last and most illustrious party to profess.

She understood these gracious disciples were her friends more than her pupils. Persuaded—perhaps by personal experience—that the heart of a young lady is a pit of turpitude and crime, she incited them to confide in her; prodding them with bizarre questions and suggestive and corrupting demands, she opened up their souls.

In exchange for the admissions she thirsted for, she offered her protection. As she had the reputation of being an altogether superior woman, the little chicks ordinarily let not just their own, private history be squeezed out, but also, and at the same time, the sordid stories of relatives and friends.

Mademoiselle du Tesson claimed to be Catholic. She did not approve of the mass, however, and spoke with lively enthusiasm of the beauties of Protestantism.

Miss Penelope lived exclusively to assure the happiness of others. This Scotswoman, having gained intelligence of the nonexistence of God, adored all the inhabitants of the planet with an equal fervor.

She was to be found on every street, on her way to offer consolation first to some, and then to others. She could not learn of a catastrophe, malady, or affliction without dashing off right away to rub on doleful or damaged parties the balm of her advice and the electuary of her compassion.

She should have wished to be everywhere at once; often, by sheer self-application, she managed to provide the illusion of ubiquity.

She would appear, at the selfsame hour, at the bedside of a dying man, at the reception of a literary immortal, on the stairwell leading to the office of a publisher or journalist, in the salon of some Jewess, at the reading of a last will and testament, or behind the bier of a defunct individual.

Thus did she thread her way—penetrating into the life of a multitude that wound up deeming her indispensable for mysterious equilibrium of some kind.

Certain parties even thought her an angel—albeit one belonging to a class uncataloged by Saint Dionysius the Areopagite and held at infinite distance from the Throne of God, in a barren steppe of the sky where rivers, living waters, and Marseille soap are all unknown.

Alas! She was an unkempt angel, and I suspect that was the little-known reason for the attraction that had put this mad planet in orbit around the stable Cleopatra, whom she deemed a star of wisdom.

It would have been difficult to decide which of the two carried the day in filthiness. It was an emulation of dirtiness, an assault of muck, a rivalry of stains and impure deposits, a competition of pulverulence, a battle of rips and tears, a tournament of exhalations from a fox's den: stale odors, stenches, and empyreumata.

The two creatures loved each other, moreover, without any blindness. Whenever the occasion arose, they judged each other with independent minds.

"That Penelope is really too dirty," du Tesson trumpeted. "She'd have to be dredged to get clean."

"I cannot conceive," piped Miss Magpie in turn, "why our dear Cleopatra neglects herself to such an extent. You'd think she wanted to inspire disgust. The administration of public roads should send a team to pick her up."

Except for that, they got on famously and their friendship was a marvel.

One important matter, however, divided them. Cleopatra advocated marriage, no matter what the altar.

"So long as one does not have a 'shared life,'" she opined, "one does not live in reality. Physically, a woman without a husband *breathes only up on top* . . ."

With great patience and a loftiness of perspective difficult to match, she expounded this thoughtworthy axiom to her islanders.

Penelope, on the other hand, declared that marriage is a state of disgrace, and the supposed necessity to sleep with a man an unbearable abomination.

The two hopeless virgins thus frequently clashed on the subject. But victory always fell to the raging Cleopatra, whose tricks crushed the objections of her adversary.

She conceded only one point: the obvious inferiority of men; this pleased Miss Magpie so greatly that discussion would end on the spot.

And so, one way or the other, it stood firm that the union of the two sexes is a physiological law—and that the horror (only too legitimate) of distinguished women for such hideous coupling only seems to be insurmountable.

"There is a lack of women who write," the doctoress vigorously concluded, "and marriage is the only way to make them. Hit or miss! Too bad if men sprout up in the process."

One day, unbeknownst to her friend, Cleopatra founded a marriage agency—a tiny little enterprise that was very discreet and only waved the torch of its offers and requests in journals with irreproachable proofreaders.

An anonymous brochure printed on pink paper informed interested parties that the *Guardian Angel of the Hearth* arranged only "unions of love." It did not deign sink to mercenary schemes, made no offers of doubtful virtue, and did not dangle fruit or light candles for adventurers.

No. The *Guardian Angel* had the sole mission of bringing together "elite hearts" that, without its mediation, would never know each other, of facilitating meetings and interviews whose innocence were guaranteed. It mustered neglected votaries of candor, lilies in the shade, and pure yet wounded souls the world does not understand. In sum, it did not lend its name to any alliances that were not completely and absolutely beyond reproach.

The noble enterprise enjoyed some success. Ancient vessels of purity who trembled with hope burst from their lairs and ran to empty their purses into Cleopatra's hands.

An austere Genevan grade-school teacher and a most agreeable old man decorated with honors received visitors and drew up the correspondence.

The founder was not involved except in difficult cases, when eloquence was necessary. Then, she was known as "Madame Aristide."

One fine day, "around the time when all is love and pullulates," Penelope—the selfsame Penelope—presented herself and requested the ideal husband, too! ...

Unfortunately, I was not present, but it seems her demands were excessive and the intervention of Madame Aristide proved necessary.

What an encounter, what a scene! Cleopatra was enraged that her anonymity had been exposed, and Penelope was furious that she and her concupiscence had been caught *in flagrante*. All at once, they unsheathed their souls—their true, shrewish souls—which were a thousand times fouler and more odious than their carcasses, and voided them on each other's head like chamber pots.

IX.   A Dentist's Terrible Punishment

"Well then, Monsieur, will you do me the honor of telling me what you desire?"

The party whom the printer addressed was an utterly generic man—the next best, in a host of insignificant and vacant individuals, to happen by; he seemed one of those people who exist *in the plural*, so fully do they express atmosphere, collectivity, and sameness: he might have said *we*, like the Pope, and he resembled an encyclical.

His face seemed to have been cast by a spade; it belonged to the innumerable number of fake he-men from the South no interbreeding can refine—but in whom everything, even the uncouthness, is just for show . . .

He could not respond then and there, for he was beside himself. At that very moment, he was making a desperate attempt to be someone. His bulging eyes rolled, full of uncertainty, and almost burst from their sockets—like the balls in games of chance that seem to pause before falling into the numbered slot where a dunce's destiny will go into fulfillment.

"Eh! Buggered buggery," he finally exclaimed in a strong Toulousan accent. "It's not like I'm looking for God's thunder in your store. I want a hundred letters announcing a wedding."

"Very well, sir. These are our models; you can choose what you like. Does *Monsieur* desire a deluxe printing on laid paper—perhaps imperial Japanese?"

"Deluxe? Gads! One doesn't get married every day. I assume you won't print it on toilet paper. Whatever's best, of course. But don't even think of adding *a black frame*, great God in Heaven!"

The printer—a simple, good-natured man on the Rue de Vaugirard—was afraid he stood in the presence of a dangerous lunatic; he contented himself to protest, under his breath, against any such oversight occurring.

When it came to wording the announcement, the customer's hand shook so violently the employee had to take dictation and write it himself:

"Monsieur Doctor Alcibiades Gerbillon has the honor to inform you of his marriage to Mademoiselle Antoinette Planchard. The nuptial benediction will be given in the parish church of Aubervilliers."

"Vaugirard and Aubervillers, that's not close at all!" thought the typographer as he gently complied.

Obviously, it wasn't close at all. For at least fifteen hours, Dr. Alcibiades Gerbillon had been wandering throughout Paris.

All the other preparations relating to the wedding to be concluded in two days he had completed quietly, like a sleepwalker. Only this formality, the announcement, had overwhelmed him. Here is why.

Gerbillon was a *murderer* who could find no rest.

If anyone is able to do so, let him explain. Having consummated his crime in the most cowardly and disgraceful manner—but without a trace of emotion, like the brute he was—he had only begun to feel remorse when he received a printed notice, conspicuously framed in black, in which an entire family in mourning entreated him to attend his victim's funeral.

This masterpiece of typography had thrown him into a panic. He was unnerved, lost: he tore out perfectly good teeth, clumsily plated insignificant stumps, assailed precious gums, and weakened jaws that had stood the test of time, inflicting terrors altogether new in kind on his clientele.

His lonesome odontologist's quarters were visited by gloomy nightmares; they ground at him even in the dentures of vulcanized rubber he planted in the orifices of distraught citizens honoring him with their trust.

And the cause of all this trouble was simply the banal message that every citizen of note in the area had welcomed with equanimity: Alcibiades was a worshiper of the Moloch of Imbeciles, whom the Printed Word grants no pardon.

Will anyone believe it? He had murdered—actually murdered—*for love.*

Justice will hold, no doubt, that such a crime should be imputed to the books the dentist read—the sole alimentation that fed this murderer's brain.

By dint of seeing how amorous situations unfold tragically in serial novels, little by little he had yielded to the temptation of removing, with a single stroke, the umbrella-merchant who blocked his good fortune.

This tradesman was young and superbly dentated—there existed no opportunity to destroy his jaw—and he was set to marry Antoinette, the daughter of Monsieur Planchard, ironmonger in bulk. Gerbillon had silently burned for her ever since he extracted a consumptive molar and the charming girl had swooned in his arms.

The banns of marriage were about to be published. With the rapidity of decision that is the greatness of dentists, Alcibiades contrived the extermination of his rival.

One morning, as torrents descended, the seller of umbrellas was found dead in his bed. Medical inspection revealed that the most dangerous species of villain had strangled the unfortunate in his sleep.

The diabolical Gerbillon, knowing better than anyone how to behave, boldly confirmed the assessment, and he felt pride at the unsparing logic of his scientific demonstration of the infamous deed. Moreover, his forensic measurements were so well taken that—following an inquest as vain as it was thorough—the law found itself obliged to give up on ever determining the guilty party.

The bloodthirsty dentist was saved, then, but not unpunished—as you will see.

Because he understood that his crime would benefit him, the umbrella-merchant's corpse was hardly lay cold before he besieged Antoinette.

The superior bearing he displayed during the inquest, the light he cast upon the obscure drama, and, finally, the respectful zeal of his tender compassion for a young lady so cruelly afflicted smoothed the path to her heart.

Truth be told, hers was not a difficult heart to obtain—it was a Babylonian heart. The ironmonger's daughter was a sensible girl in good health, and she wasted herself but little on grief.

She held no pretentions to the vainglory of eternal lamentation and made no point of being beyond consolation.

"One doesn't live for the dead; one husband lost, ten gained"—and so on—Alcibiades whispered. A few maxims pulled out from the same pit soon revealed the nobility of this man who lied through his teeth. He seemed transcendent to her.

"It is your heart, Mademoiselle, I should like to uproot," he said one day. A decisive proclamation.

These charming words—which, fortunately, the girl's upbringing let her savor—made up her mind. Moreover, Gerbillon was a groom who was fit to be seen. Agreement was easily reached, and the marriage occurred.

Yet why must happiness obtained at such expense be poisoned by memory of the dead? Did the famous letter of mourning, whose impression had started to fade, not reappear in the imagination of the murderer who stupidly thought it had denounced him? The evening before his wedding—as has just been seen—the obsession had come back, more vigorous than before; it pushed him into madness and caused him to wander like a fugitive for a whole day in Paris, where he did not live—until the terrible hour he finally mustered the energy to order the announcements from the Vaugirard printer (who surely had guessed his crime).

What was the use of having been so clever and resourceful, of throwing the law off the track so well, and of obtaining, against all hope, the hand of a woman he idolized—only to succumb to the misery of recurring hallucinations!

The first days' intoxication was but a respite. The fine horns of the newly-weds' crescent honeymoon were not yet done piercing the azure sky when a germ of tribulation sprouted.

One morning, Alcibiades discovered the umbrella-salesman's portrait. Well! It was just a photograph that Antoinette had innocently accepted back when she thought they were to be married.

Outraged and furious, the dentist immediately tore it to pieces before his wife's eyes; even though the relic did not strike her as particularly precious, the violence repulsed her.

Yet at the same time—because nothing at all can be destroyed—the hostile image that had existed only on paper, as the visible reflection of a fragment of the indiscernible photographic snapshot enveloping the universe, became fixed in the memory—which now, suddenly, was *impressed*—of Madame Gerbillon.

Henceforth haunted by the deceased, whose memory had nearly grown indifferent to her, she saw only him. She saw him without cease. She breathed him in and breathed him out through all her pores. With all her effluvia, she saturated her sad husband with him; he, in turn, was surprised and distressed always to find the corpse between them.

At the end of the year, they had an epileptic child—a monstrous male child with the face of a thirty-year-old who prodigiously resembled the man Gerbillon had murdered.

The father fled screaming. He wandered about like a madman for three days. On the fourth evening of the fourth day, he bent over his son's cradle and strangled him, choked by sobs.

X. The Awakening of Alain Chartier

My Dear *Friend*,

Come tonight at eleven o'clock. The door to the garden will be ajar. Just push it gently. I'll be waiting for you under the bower. My husband is gone for two days, and he took the dog with him. Too bad if I am lost. I love you and wish to be yours.

ROLANDE

Upon receiving this *billet*, young Duputois went so pale his colleagues suspected some disaster. He was extremely discreet and scrupulously hid the message in the most mysterious corner of his wallet; stuttering a little, he spoke of a creditor's threat.

Yet it was impossible to get back to work. Reading these few lines had broken him, crumbled him into bits. He experienced the physical unwellness of a man who has not eaten for two days: an empty head, painful joints, and fever. A brand burned the pit of his stomach, his heart beat intolerably, and a hysterical bubble blocked his esophagus.

It is banal to mention the troubles occasioned by love in young people, and even in old ones. They are the sensations of the condemned being dragged off to the guillotine. Such intimate connections hold between the latter and sensual pleasures that in certain towns during the Middle Ages the aldermen and burgomasters ordered that the executioner's lair should be located in lowly alleys where prostitution encamped. Bawds "of the great woode," as Panurge says, must occasionally have made a wrong turn.

Florimond Duputois was not young enough to practice psychology. A few days earlier, he had passed twenty years, and self-analysis did not occur to him.

He simply observed that the skin of his skull gave him awful pain and his legs were like jelly. He tried to drink several times, but the water from the office pitcher seemed to have the aftertaste of carrion.

"After all," he asked himself, "why this letter? I've done nothing, really, to attract her—this pretty woman. I've spoken with her directly two times at most, and I'm altogether certain she must have thought me an idiot. But it's true I'm not more unappetizing than the next man—especially when I recite verses after dinner. I can imagine full well that a lady, at that particular instant, might get carried away, feel a passing fancy. My God! Yes, why not? Yet all the same, the letter's a little stiff, and truly I find the preliminaries wanting for a rendezvous."

He moralized to himself all day, remonstrating most wisely, for the young man drew his sustenance exclusively from the roots of virtue.

The husband was an old friend of the family, whose protection had proven advantageous. He owed him his employment at the ministry, the promise of a brilliant future, as well as a reasonably large number of agreeable acquaintances; he also dined at his house several times a month. One could not make a cuckold of this man without plunging headfirst into a well of filth. It meant certain and absolute dishonor, the lowest and most fetid of actions, betrayal to make one hang one's head forevermore, and so on.

And so, in consequence, he arrived at the gracious resolution to attend the rendezvous with utmost punctuality.

Yes, indeed. He'd go and see what he was made of. He'd talk sense to this neglected wife who was ready to sacrifice her honor to him. He'd make her appreciate the enormity of her mistake and the terrible disadvantages such a dangerous liaison would entail.

Ultimately, he'd hand her back to her husband, casting her into the ever-welcoming arms of that man of character—who would never know that the greatest of outrages had stood so very near.

Soon, he was aglow with passion to repay his benefactor's charitable deeds in this manner.

Ah! How lucky *the dear creature* was to have encountered him! She could just as well have given herself to some imbecile or boor who would not have thought twice about abusing the situation and bringing still lower this drooping flower, who so needed a helping hand to be uplifted . . .

How many others, in his place, would see nothing but the opportunity to satisfy their dirty instincts, to exult in their peacock-pride; beyond all doubt, they would already have shouted from the rooftops the fall of a poor, lost woman, the victim of her own enthusiasm! . . .

I have neglected to mention that Florimond Duputois had a stub nose, eyes like soup ladles, the mouth of a lepidopteran, scaly skin, and low-slung hindquarters; he was also mortally afraid of cows.

Allow me to observe that he belonged to the Symbolist pleiade and regularly contributed to *Grimoire, Melusina,* and the *Revue of the Rattlesnakes.*

A little before the appointed hour, he hurried from the office, ran to the coiffeur to be adonized, took a reincarnating meal, and reread a few pages of "Afternoon of a Faun" to elevate his heart; then, finally sure of himself, he boarded the omnibus on the Auteuil line.

Indeed, the little door to Madame Rolande's garden stood ajar. When, with infinite precaution, he gave it a push, it opened little by little onto a black abyss. The alley, scarcely visible from the threshold, immediately vanished among the deep plantings.

Since he had often been admitted to stroll his inspiration through this labyrinth, he knew, as the saying goes, all its winding ways.

As he closed the door behind him, he proceeded with a processional air, seized again by all his confusion. The great bell within his heart pealed wildly.

The silence stood as deep as any lawbreaker might wish or fear—here, in a sedate district inhabited only by the ill and estimable millionaires.

Faintly, at some distance toward the morning's light, stirred vague murmurs and the prolonged lamentation of one of Maldoror's melancholy hounds, tormented by the infinite . . .

As he approached the bower of aristolochia and woodbine where the guilty wife awaited him, his confidence diminished, his step grew less certain, and his trembling became more difficult to suppress. Finally, his teeth chattered with such force he feared it would wake the slumbering birds; he felt himself grow so pale he wondered if he would tint the leaves with his pallor, like a phosphorescent fish.

All of a sudden, a hand rested on his shoulder.

"Here I am, dearly beloved," said Madame Rolande's voice.

And almost as soon, the woman's arms fastened about his neck; a kiss of life-or-death consumed his soul.

Ah! What a voracious and savage kiss it was! The young man had anticipated everything—except for this fiery, insatiable, and eternal kiss. It was fragrant and heady, commingling all the fierce perfumes of the *Flowers of Evil*: the disorienting scents of Venison and the awful piquancy of Desire. This kiss had talons like an eagle and hunted like a lion; it penetrated him like a sword of fire; it filled his ears with the ringing bells of alpine goats and rams; this dreadful kiss: opium, raging madness, stupefaction, and ecstasy!

His chaste desires cleared out. They'd gone to the Devil, to God's thunder, and down a crack on the Moon's surface (along with the Orphic harangues and objurgations previously mentioned).

Duputois was bobbing in the depths when he heard the sound of a footstep. The darkness was absolute; he couldn't make anything out at all.

Thereupon, the lyric poet of the *Revue of the Rattlesnakes* was struck, square in the face, by two furious palms that sent him reeling, almost to the ground.

Ridding herself of the poor devil, Madame Rolande had leapt backward. Now he heard two people whispering as they quickly gained the house.

He was afraid to breathe and dared not budge from his station, and so, for an hour, he stood still in the darkness, not knowing what to hope for.

But finally, worn down by fatigue and frozen by the starlight, he found his way to the garden door, still ajar, and to the well-known sidewalk of dejected souls. He had made no more sound than a black ant wandering off into the black night—just as crestfallen and stiff as a youth full of soliloquies and prosody can be.

The following day, he was summoned to the antechamber of the ministry. He found himself in the presence of a very handsome and reasonably athletic man, who had the air of a cavalry officer with the most exquisite manners. He addressed him in these terms:

"Monsieur, an error of address put in your hands a woman's note that was intended for me. It is useless, I think, to mention the contents of the message. Indeed, I ask that you scrupulously forget them. Having received, for my part, the few lines meant to reach you, I made the fortunate conjecture that the addresses had been switched, and was therefore able to arrive just in time to avert disaster. You are known as a gallant man, and I count that, in exchange for this letter here, you will immediately restore the autograph belonging to me. I add, Monsieur Poet (altogether unnecessarily, I am sure), that *the mistress of Caesar stands above suspicion.*"

The last phrase, which was only too clear, received such significant emphasis that the puny boy, who was incapable of expectorating so much as a diphthong, did as requested.

Behold the contents of the other missive:

Monsieur Duputois, I would be infinitely obliged were you, in the future, to agree to spare me the honor of receiving your dedications in little journals. Your poems are exquisite, I am sure, yet I confess that I prefer humble prose; the role of muse does not suit me. Yours, etc.

This trifling adventure occurred in 187. . . . Enjoying greater and greater preferment, Florimond Duputois has continued his songs at the ministry. We are reliably informed he will receive the knighthood next 14 July.

XI. The Stroker of Compassion

I met him in 1864, when he was barely a youth. We lived together for more than twenty years, and I loved him as one rarely loves a brother.

Today, now that the unfortunate man has descended a bit lower than the dead, I can well say I was a most diligent, attentive, and devotional teacher.

Everything good in his poor soul—which now lies as barren as the granaries of Famine—he received from my lips; he was fed like the hatchlings of nightbirds, terrified of the light.

From the lamp at the altars—the lamp that never goes out—I borrowed the tranquil and upright flame necessary to disobstruct a mind that naturally weaves darkness.

Being the elder, I set him upon my shoulders. For a third of my sad life, I held him in the stained glass of distant horizons; each day, as I grew myself, I lifted him a little farther out of the mud, and I will ache forever for having borne him.

I'd have been loath to complain, however. I was sure I had wrested prey from the Demon of Folly—prey all the more precious for seeming to have been destined, in advance and by its very origin, to the Catcher of the Masses.

Nemorin Thierry had been plucked from a low branch on the medlar of the Bourgeoisie, whose fruits rot as soon as they touch the ground. Consequently, he received from the authors of his days a mind that gaped for mediocre ideas and recoiled at all impressions of a higher order.

His education proved worse than difficult, and it required continuous exertion. On the one hand, it was a matter of stopping up a hole; on the other, it involved digging little ditches for irrigation, weeding the soil, transplanting wild growth, clearing off pests, and pruning—all at once.

It was imperative to draw this poor being outside of himself, to sift and filter him—in short, to set up and fashion, one way or the other, a little spirit for him, something more alive that would, little by little, take away his identity.

In appearance, the results were such that I may be pardoned for having viewed myself as a thaumaturgist—up to forgetting the formal law that beasts and plants whose cultivation is interrupted regress to their rudimentary type.

Mine was the misfortune not to hear the incessant reminders of the primeval and indestructible rose hip.

In a word, I believed that poor Nemorin could walk on his own; having propped him up for twenty years, I committed the irreparable imprudence of setting him down on the ground.

I don't know how to muster the force to say what he became. Could I have guessed that such great efforts would be so completely and abominably lost—from the first day on—and yield nothing other than infinite bitterness when I finally admitted they had been useless?

He was called Sweet Thierry, and without a hint of irony. He was as soft as the down of doves, as mild as holy oils, and as gentle as the Moon.

No one should suspect me of exaggerating. Truly, he was so sweet nobody could imagine an individual belonging to the male sex—and consequently summoned to reproduce the species—sweeter than him.

He melted like chocolate in one's hand, calmed all waters, and called to mind the silkiest cocoons of caterpillars. Nothing made him angry or roused his indignation; his teacher, who was sworn to masculinize this void, despaired at never getting anything from him but the palest glow—no matter how furiously his gelatinous conscience was stoked or fanned.

Several times, I tried to reassure myself by supposing him one of those natures I demand permission to call *Eucharistic*—"soaked with ambrosia and honey," in Chenier's words—whose power consists precisely in enduring everything, who seem to have been placed at the edges of the human soil to dampen shocks and collisions.

Yet such a state may not be supposed unless it is accompanied by theological predestination; unfortunately—and as I recognized only too late—certain appetitions or obscure inclinations absolutely eliminate the hypothesis of the "elect vessel" with which my magisterial gullibility contented itself.

Sweet Thierry was simply a little pig, and he belonged to the race of Strokers of Compassion (who hardly dominate the world).

When did he start to stroke and compassionate? In what April of baneful germination did this cleft penchant suddenly develop? God only knows. He himself could probably not have said—even when he still seemed able to speak, to voice sounds that were actually human.

I do know that one fine day, he found he was perfectly equipped to exercise his functions. Exchanges on the omnibus, dairies well stocked with little women at work, the vestibules of train stations, and even churches were his preferred sporting ground.

Permeated by the idea that he absolutely required a female companion, he desired a *simple* one, above all; from then on—and as a matter of consequence as necessary as the course of the heavens—his ancestors' albumen strictly demanded that sentimental vulgarity ever shape the object of his heart's election.

Appalling, smirking little examples of defilement struck him as singularly as the light of the Empyrean. Yet their number was so great he never could manage to focus his dilection on just one.

A Don Juan whom mature errand girls and galvanoplastic dressmakers served as guardians, he assiduously sought the ideal Object from among the crowds.

With marvelous patience, which no setback could unsettle, he fervently sought a professional mourner at whose breast he could lay his brow, naked and abounding in clemency, like a spray of mimosas.

Though he was little gifted in a physiological sense, he experienced keen pulsations of love; no doubt, he made claim to joys of a lower order but rarely.

What intoxicated, delighted, and disoppilated him, shook his soul with extreme pleasures and spread his entire person with the unguent and olibanum of beatitudinous languor, was *to barely touch*, to palpitate ever so slightly, to graze here and there—like the tip of a butterfly's wing—with his tactile organ; all the while, he would exhale melodious and piteous moans about the sad fate of the lilies of the valley and wilted bindweed that indelicate adventurers of luxuriance trampled underfoot.

Such noble constancy was to be rewarded. Descending from the heavens one day, Beatrice appeared.

You may laugh as much as you wish, but that's how it was. She really was called Beatrice, and she worked the sewing machine for a living.

Nemorin met her in a soup kitchen; for seven years, he rubbed up without wearying. True, his innermost feeling spilled out on the intercalary occasions his verve unfortunately demanded; it is not permitted to disregard one's vocation altogether.

For her part, Beatrice seemed to have no desire to keep him entirely for herself, and she even attempted, spring and autumn, to dismiss the lachrymose twiddler who clung to her.

No matter. She was the Ideal all the same, and death alone could set her free.

How many times, when I was still trying to rein him in—how many times, merciful heavens, and with what eyes flooded with the Infinite—did he speak of her to me; thus did the first Christians, under the tooth of beasts, speak of their God!

At any rate, I'll say it again: this liturgy of little thrills and soft sighs allowed the Earth to complete its course around the Sun seven times.

"Is she at least your mistress?" I would sometimes ask.

It was a brutal question, I admit, and it promptly made him clamber back up into his stained-glass window. His response in the negative then expired in a pious gesture.

Need I say it? Beatrice stank at the mouth—and probably from her big feet, too. She was so dumb that after talking to her for half an hour, you felt she was sprouting a wattle.

Her manners suited her face. One might have thought it had been pulled out of a common pork butcher's salting tub.

At the same time, she was irritable enough to make dogs abort. As prudish as arithmetic, she welcomed in her so-very-pure bed, without too much fuss, the crepuscular suffrages of a few worn-out goats employed in petty commerce.

Six times out of ten, Sweet Thierry had to choke down his tears upon finding her door closed. It even happened that he nearly wound up getting thrown down the stairs beneath a torrent of the filthiest curses. Even though it saddened him, violence of the kind still seemed to derive from a soul altogether divine; naturally, it quadrupled his ardor.

"She has suffered so much!" he said, clasping his hands to the azure so that it might bear witness.

Incidentally, Beatrice would collect his worshipful tribute in the form of dinners and little presents; then, the following day, she would clarify the situation.

Some five hundred times, this bottom-of-the-barrel strumpet had made him swallow—in another phrasing, no doubt, yet how easily!—the famous words of a dazzling courtesan: "You don't love me anymore! You believe what you see and don't believe what I tell you!"

In the sublime exaltation of his faith, Nemorin learned matters that only confounded me.

"*She explained everything!*" he said one day; a few hours earlier, he had noticed at his beloved's lodgings a pair of men's slippers and a rack of pipes—most of them *seasoned* (much more, no doubt, than the location suggested). She had explained everything! . . .

But now? Ah! Now, it's death he strokes—an abject death, I assure you. It's the horrible death that demands no compassion and never offers any, either. Death that oozes . . .

My God! my God! Once I had held him in my arms—this child of the Void, this son of Non-Existence, this twin of Insignificance and Illusion I hoped to fashion into a living being!

I had sought to breathe my soul into him. For him, I labored, suffered, prayed, cried, and sobbed—for years, the dearest and most precious years of my life!

I had taken dreadful burdens upon myself he would never have had the strength to bear. All a man can do, truly I believe I did.

To arm him against the assignations of nothingness, I had presented—unfurled before him—images that never fade; I had wiped myself out painting realities that can know no end . . . I didn't even manage to make riffraff out of him . . .

And now, today, he repeats a senile request from dawn to dusk: not to have a *cross* planted on his grave. Feeding him with a little tin spoon, one must hold up his lower lip, so the mush won't spill.

XII. Monsieur's Past

> Penetrate, my heart,
> Into this charming past.
> VICTOR HUGO

"Eighty thousand francs, sir! That's some nerve. So you've come a hundred leagues to ask that of me? You thought I'd jump at the chance to deprive my wife and the children I may yet have to pay for that little hussy's escapades? I don't recognize her as my niece at all—I disown her, you hear me well! Well then, you must take me for a sucker. Eighty thousand francs! Why not a million while you're at it?"

Fifteen years ago, a heavyset wine grower of Lower Charente addressed these thoughtful words to me; his broad face looked like a baboon's hindquarters.

I can't say that I had had a great deal of confidence when seeking out the extremely wealthy wine merchant, whom I did not know previously. Only too well was I aware of the proverbial poverty of millionaires—and of their appallingly bad luck, which ensures that only the slightest bit of what they possess ever stands at their disposal whenever one happens to approach them.

All the same, the sheer enormity of the sum to be obtained had made me hope for at least a little consideration. But from the first glance, I had the fatal presentiment of failure; I had only taken the matter on in order to set my conscience at ease.

Truly, the affair was a most singular one. It meant instilling in this barrel of a man a specific quantity of familial disinterest perhaps equal to the tenth part of one million; to be sure, I was an ill-suited ambassador for negotiations of the kind.

"By God, sir!" I replied, "Truly, you're most amiable for not setting your dogs on me right away or calling the police. Thus, I make bold to remind you I'm acting in the name of the dead—that is, obeying the last wishes of an unfortunate girl buried only the day before last. In all this, as you can well see, I am but a representative, one who has taken great bother upon himself. You are free to do nothing—even to deny, as much as you like, your own flesh and blood. However, the voyage has tired me greatly; I'm astonished you haven't made even a slight show of hospitality."

These words, aiming to prolong the interview by a few hours, during which I would endeavor to snare my host, did not displease him. He softened—grew cordial, even—and invited me to lunch.

Still, as engaging and suggestive as the viticulturer's table was, my diplomatic subtleties and compassionating eloquence proved as inefficacious as I had anticipated. I took away nothing from the visit but a bitter confirmation of my powerlessness to penetrate the carapace of hippopotamuses and pachydermic philosophers.

The niece's story is perhaps the most extraordinarily lamentable sequence of events I have encountered. Her name was Justine D . . . , and she died at the age of twenty-eight in the most terrible despair.

A third of her *too lengthy* existence she devoted, exclusively and in vain, to winning a wretched man she had judged superior—a man whom she adored to a criminal extent, and whose wife she wished to be, whatever the cost. Surely our fin-de-siècle—spindly and spiraliform, like a pig's tail—offers few examples of enchantment like this.

The miracle is that this flower of passion, this *passiflora incarnata*, had grown in utterly inhospitable soil, under the most unfavorable conditions that one can imagine.

She was one of those virgins on a string—the kind prepared in the fabric business or in the trade of salted meats—who spring from the estimable rib of a merchant who always pays his bills in full.

Consequently, she was raised in wise horror of constellations and glowing glories; naturally, one would have supposed nothing to be straighter than her sentiments and transports.

Her heart had been cultivated like a small-scale vegetable garden, where the slightest beds are calculated for making a stew. There were no useless flowers (whose frivolous display yields no gain). At the very most, room had been made for a few violets abutting the beans and lettuce, lest poetry wind up altogether exiled.

Two or three odd volumes of Emile Souvestre and the great Dumas, an anthology of poetic dainties, and the daily intake of local news items in the *Petit Journal* more than satisfied her hunger for literature.

In a word, never had a girl seemed more fully destined to become the ornament and reward of an "honest man."

I shall undertake to explain neither miracles nor mysteries, and one should not expect psychological elucidation of the events I mean to narrate. They are only too real.

What is certain is that the tree yielded fruits no longer permitting that the source be recognized, and the tiny vegetable garden brought forth strange flowers—exotic ones, probably—precisely where turnips or potatoes were expected.

All of a sudden, a heroine—a veritable, scandalous heroine of love— shone forth in our Justine, the girl deemed worthy only to rise to the height of sustaining a man in commerce.

Except that, lest nature renounce all its rights, the man she loved so much more than life itself was a mediocrity among mediocrities—a blond clerk who scraped out high-pitched notes on his voice, built foamy little landscapes in the bathtub, and, still at the age of thirty, sported the gentle down of an adolescent.

This basilisk of salesgirls offered her sublime Illusion. Behold the unbelievable drama that ensued.

Narcissus Lepinoche—for such was the conqueror's name—did not refuse to marry Justine in the least. After all, she was as good as any other. However, since he had no capital apart from his job and the payments he was obliged to make to usurers, and because he wanted, on top of that, to cast his nets for a little longer, he showed no great hurry to bind to his own the existence of a young girl who didn't have a cent and whose beauty was not especially overpowering.

I never thought him squalid, but heroic disinterest was not his line. Inasmuch as one spoke of "making a home," didn't basic foresight dictate they should, at very least, wait for an inheritance from uncle Tiburtius? He and his beanpoles made a hundred thousand francs a year; nor could one doubt that he wouldn't be long in quitting the world where his beautiful soul was still exiled.

In fact, and for some time now, Justine had been ruined by her dunce of a father, who had invested his entire fortune in blasting a notorious tunnel through the Himalayas, meant to connect English India to Manchuria.

The colossal failure of the venture had cast the speculator into the deepest of pits, and the young girl lived with her mother upon the miserable debris of erstwhile opulence, clinging to the hope that a fortunate inheritance would unite her person to her dear Lepinoche; from one day to the next, he struck her as more and more handsome and worthy of her idolatry.

After all, he was her uncle—her father's own brother—this Tiburtius of wines and spirits; he was known to be very rich and very miserly, yet he was old and had no children. In keeping with earlier custom, he would send a case of bottles once a year. That was all. Alas, one just had to wait: this man would prove useful only in the manner of pigs—that is, after death.

As bad luck had it, the skinflint seemed not to want to die, and so the years passed by. Justine found herself growing old, even though she fought with rage. For his part, Lepinoche had visibly lost his appetite, and he hardly made it a secret that he was looking elsewhere.

He even grew impertinent. I never learned the details or the full scope of events, but one may be sure that the poor girl was altogether incensed for never having refused anything to her wretched beloved. On more than one occasion, I believe I had occasion to observe the latter's mean spirit—the cowardly cruelty of a dandy there's no point in even approaching, a man who has given nothing in return for getting it all.

𓆰

One day I was besought, with great urgency, on behalf of the unfortunate creature. Before dying, she wanted to speak to me alone.

The priest I met on the stairwell seemed glad I had come. He looked very pale and assured me that my presence would relieve him of a great burden. Then he departed, imploring me to be *charitable*.

I had just come back from a long voyage, and so I hadn't seen Justine for several months. It was hard to recognize her—she had grown so beautiful in the claws of death.

I could see only her eyes—what eyes!—in a face entirely white but for moving shadows and light, as if a torch were passing before her.

Her lips had lost all color and were visible only in contrast to the dark line of her teeth, blackened by fever. The rest was indistinct—melted and fused into whiteness that practically gleamed; it was almost luminous: the white of polished alabaster shining through a blanket of snow! Her hair was pulled back and disappeared in dark abundance.

I'm sure I didn't feel anything but pity at the time—the most heart-rending pity of my life—and especially when she spoke to me. Only later was I to perceive the supernatural beauty in this composition of Horror and Pain.

She was waiting for me, sitting upright in bed.

"Monsieur," she said in a very low voice, "I have just received last rites, and I am going to die . . . God is very good. I hope He will not deny me . . . I have asked you to come because you are a true friend; you will fulfill, I am sure, the humble request of a desolate heart.

"Except for the priest who has just left, no one knows what I have done yet. When I am dead, the whole world will learn, and the disgrace will be awful . . .

"I have ruined several people who trusted me. I deceived them contemptibly. For three years, my life was nothing but imposture—a lie every day, a lie every hour. I made old family friends think we were not bankrupt, my mother and I. They lent me substantial sums; I speculated with them and lost. Without knowing a thing about it, but with the stubbornness of the damned, I traded on the stock exchange in the hope of making a fortune . . . You understand . . . I wanted to make myself rich for the man I loved to my soul's perdition—whom I still love, and for whom I am dying *to no end*!

". . . I robbed very poor people. Once, monsieur, I took from an old woman, who was infirm and nearly blind, the few titles and credit slips in her possession; I substituted brochures printed on gaudy paper . . . This Christian soul, who cherished me, will be forced to beg for her bread.

"Because I always lost, I was prepared to commit any crime in the false hope that I might regain the money . . . Anyway, I owe more than EIGHTY THOUSAND FRANCS! Only my uncle could pay it—my rich uncle, whose death I have so often desired. Go find him, I beg you, as soon as I am put into the earth; tell him *it is I who am dying*—that I am dying in horror of all these curses on my miserable grave! . . . In horror! . . ."

The dying woman let out a great cry and, casting her arms about my neck, barked these final words, which I still can hear:

"Ah! If you knew . . . , if you knew what I see! . . ."

It was finished. I was forced to extract myself from the corpse's embrace; the nails had pierced my skin, and the eyes, incredibly dilated, were still staring . . .

The uncle, of course, didn't pay a thing, and Lepinoche, when I told him how she had died a little later, confided that he found the whole matter quite sad, really.

Four years later, he married the daughter of a well-situated flunkey about town. She is a respectable woman who frowns on excess of any kind and no longer permits him to see me.

XIII.   Whatever You Want! . . .

Maxentius, tired from a long evening of pleasure, reached the corner where Dupleix, the street and the alley, meet opposite the École Militaire. Merely vile by day, the spot was rather sinister at night—that night, at one o'clock in the morning. The black alley in particular seemed less than reassuring. The stretch of muddy road, where artillery- and cavalrymen were serviced at a base price in fearsome barracks, disquieted the nighttime walker.

All the same, he weighed his options. A murmur was rumbling from the direction of Boulevard de Grenelle, which wise men dread. Because he didn't want to stumble into some kind of trouble with drunkards, he was inclined to steer down the dirty passageway; standing at one end of it, he thought it would surely provide a more peaceable valley for following the course of his amorous reveries.

Coming from his mistress's arms, he felt the need to dissipate his dissipation in the drowsiness of an unmolested voyage home.

"Well, then! What'll it be?" asked a despicable voice trying hard to seem kindly.

Maxentius witnessed a heavyset woman detach from the nearest wall and come to make the precious offering of her love.

"I won't charge much, either; come on, I'll do whatever you want, dearie."

She unfolded the menu. The paralyzed stroller heard every word as if he were listening to his own heart beating. It was stupid, of course, but for some reason the voice moved him. The poor man couldn't have said why—

even if his very life had depended on it. Anyway, his unease was plenty certain . . . And it turned into intolerable anguish as soon as he felt that his soul was being dragged off by the disgraceful sales talk; like an ebbing tide, it carried him back to the most distant waters of the past.

How unspeakably the apparition profaned memories of marvelous sweetness! His childhood impressions had something divine about them—alas, his current life could boast of little glory.

Whenever he sought to gather his wits after painting the town red, he called upon them; then, the impressions would trot back, compliantly and dutifully—like timid sheep that had been lost and wanted nothing more than simply to follow their pastor . . .

But this time, he had not called for them. They had come on their own—or rather, *another voice* had called them, a voice they heeded, no doubt, as much as his own. It was horrifying not to understand what was occurring.

"*Whatever you want!* I'll do whatever you want, sweetheart . . ."

Truly, it was intolerable. His mother was dead; she had been burnt alive in a fire. He remembered a carbonized hand—the only part of her corpse they had dared show him.

His only sister—fifteen years his senior, who had raised him with such care, and to whom he owed his best qualities—had met an equally tragic end. Off one of the most inhospitable coasts of the Gulf of Gascony, the ocean had swallowed her along with fifty other passengers, men and women, in a shipwreck that was only too notorious. It had proved impossible to recover her body.

These two dolorous creatures possessed him whenever he rested on his elbow and beheld the flow of his life from the parapet of Memory.

Well! It was terrible, it was monstrous, but this beggar who now detained him there on the sidewalk—on this embankment of Hell, as Maeterlinck would say—spoke with exactly the same voice as his sister, that creature of election who seemed to belong to the angelic host, whose feet, he believed, would have purified the muds of Sodom.

Alas, there could be no doubt! It was her voice: inexpressibly degraded, fallen from the sky, and rolled in dirty pits where the thunders perish. But it was her voice all the same—so much so that he was tempted to run off sobbing and crying.

Thus is it true that the dead can slip in among the living—or among those who pretend to be!

At the very instant the old prostitute promised her hideous flesh to him—and in what manner, Heavens above!—he heard his sister, whom the fish had devoured a quarter of a century earlier, commending him to love God and the poor.

"If only you saw how pretty my thighs are!" said the vampire.

"If only you knew the beauty of Jesus!" said the saint.

"Come up to my place, naughty boy. I've made a nice fire and a nice bed. You won't regret it," the one started up.

"Do not wrong your guardian angel," murmured the other.

Involuntarily, he pronounced *out loud* the pious recommendation that once had filled his childhood completely.

At these words, the petitioner experienced a shock and began to tremble. Lifting her runny, old, bloodshot eyes—extinguished mirrors that seemed to reflect every scene of debauchery and every image of torture—she fixed him hungrily with the terrifying stare of the drowned contemplating, one last time, the glaucous sky through the window of the water that asphyxiates them . . .

A moment of silence passed.

"Monsieur," she finally said, "I ask your pardon. I was wrong to approach you. I'm nothing but an old hag—a mattress for lowlifes—and you should have kicked me into the gutter. Go back to your home and *may the Lord keep you.*"

Maxentius was overwhelmed as he watched her promptly vanish into darkness.

๛

She was right, after all. He had to get back. And so, after this delay, he directed his course back toward Boulevard de Grenelle—but how slowly! The encounter had all but knocked him out.

He hadn't yet made ten steps when the old eater-of-brains reappeared, running after him.

"Monsieur, I beg of you, don't go that way."

"Why shouldn't I?" he asked. "It's the path I take—I live on Vaugirard."

"Too bad. You should retrace your steps, make a detour—even if it adds an hour. You risk getting a beating if you cross the boulevard. If you must know, half the pimps of Paris have gathered there to do business. They're all the way from the slaughterhouses up to the tobacco plant. The police have left them the whole street. You wouldn't have anybody to protect you, and they'll strike a hard bargain."

Maxentius was tempted to respond that he had no need of protection; fortunately, however, he sensed the folly of such bravado.

"Fine," he said. "I'll go back up by the Invalides. All the same, it's a bit much. I'm exhausted; this extra hike, on top of it all, is exasperating. They should set the cavalry on those panderers . . ."

"There might be a way," the old woman said after a moment of hesitation.

"Ah! Let's hear it."

Then, quite humbly, she submitted that, being well known in this agreeable milieu, it would be easy for her to conduct someone . . .

"Except," she added with surprising mildness, "they would have to believe you're an . . . acquaintance—and for that, you'd have to let me take your arm."

Now it was Maxentius's turn to waver. He feared a trap of some kind. But an unknown force stirred within him, and his hesitation proved brief. And so he managed to traverse the foul crowd without injury because he held, on his arm and near his heart, this creature greeted by several bandits on the way—a figure to dispirit even Sin itself.

Not a word passed between them. He simply noted that she clutched his arm, pushing up against him much more than the situation required, strictly speaking—and also that there was something convulsive about this grip.

The extraordinary confusion he felt dissipated now that she was no longer speaking. Naturally, he wound up supposing that it had all been some kind of *hallucination*. Everyone knows how convenient this precious word is: it clears up all dark sentiments—or presentiments.

※

When the time came to part, Maxentius formulated some banal expression of gratitude and took out his wallet, meaning to reward the strange, silent companion who perhaps had just saved him.

But she stopped him with a gesture:

"No, monsieur, not that."

Then he saw that she was crying. For the whole half-hour they had walked together, he had not dared looked at her.

"What's wrong?" he asked, quite moved. "What can I do for you?"

"If you let me kiss you," she replied, "it would be the greatest joy of my disgusting life; after that, I think I would have the courage to die."

Seeing that he gave his assent, she pounced. Growling with love, she kissed him as if she were devouring him.

A groan from the smothered man caused her to draw away.

"Farewell, Maxentius, little Maxentius, my poor brother. Farewell forever—and forgive me!" she cried. "Now I can die."

Before her brother had the time to make the slightest movement, her head was crushed beneath the wheels of a *dump* truck that rushed past like a storm.

Maxentius no longer has a mistress. At the moment, he is finishing his novitiate as a lay brother at the Grande Chartreuse.

XIV. Well-Done

> Death lasts
> For a long time.
>
> AN HEIR

Monsieur Fiacre-Prétextat Labalbarie retired from affairs at the age of sixty, having amassed considerable riches in the coffin-blanching business.

He had never disappointed his clients. The Genevan aristocracy, which had inundated him with orders for so long, celebrated his precision and dedication in a single voice.

The excellence of his handiwork, attested even by wary England, had received the endorsements of Belgium, Illinois, and Michigan.

And so, it occasioned great bitterness in both worlds when international journals despairingly announced that the famous artisan was abandoning the ceremonies of commerce in order to devote his venerable white temples to studies dear to his heart.

Indeed, Fiacre was a happy old man; his philosophical and humanitarian calling did not make itself known until the moment that fortune—which is much less blind and, no doubt, much less nasty than the vain multitude supposes—finally showered him with its favors.

He did not at all contemn, as so may do, the infinitely honorable and lucrative trade that had enabled him to rise from almost nothing up to the height of some ten millions.

On the contrary, with the naïve enthusiasm of an old soldier he recounted the innumerable battles he had waged against rivals, and he boastfully recalled the gunfire—which had indeed proven heroic on occasion—of his inventories.

Following the example of Charles V, he simply abdicated the imperial throne of the invoice in order to embrace a higher life.

He possessed sufficient means to live, and he had grown too old to pretend for much longer that he might preserve the discerning gaze of a businessman—that spontaneous *something*, which tips the balance and undoes competitors' schemes. Accordingly, he had the wisdom to resign from commercial power while still at an advantage, before the star of his trade license began to fade.

Henceforth, he devoted himself exclusively to the benefaction of mankind. With a touching clarity of vision, he contemplated the nullity of all contrivances that empty heads had devised until now to attenuate poverty. Moreover, being unshakably convinced of the *utility* of the poor, he thought better than to employ the financial and intellectual resources at his disposal in order to relieve the woes of this herd.

Consequently, he resolved to apply the last glimmers of his genius to the consolation of millionaires.

"Who," he asked, "thinks of how the rich suffer? Perhaps I alone do (along with the divine Bourget, whom my clients adore). Because they fulfill their mission—which involves amusing themselves in order to make commerce thrive—they are too easily supposed happy. One forgets that they have a heart. Outrageously, their ills are set in opposition to the uncouth tribulations of the indigent—whose duty, after all, is to suffer. As if rags and the want of food were equal to the anguish of dying! For such is the law: one cannot truly perish unless one owns something. Capital is indispensable for giving up the ghost, and that's what no one appreciates. Death is nothing but separation from Money. Those who don't have anything also don't have any life; ergo, they cannot die."

Full of such thoughts—which are deeper than he suspected—the bleacher of coffins poured his very soul into abolishing the torments of death.

He had the distinction of being one of the very first advocates of the charitable idea of Cremation. According to this thinker, the traditional fear of death follows above all from the horrifying image of decomposition. In the Curiate Assembly of Incineration that elected him President, he described its stages and elucidated—with the eloquence of terror—all of its subterranean chemistry. The thought of becoming a flower, for example, repulsed this accountant's imagination.

His wishes were wholly granted, as you will see.

The estimable gentleman had a son such as one might wish upon all who know what money is worth.

May I be granted leave to digress for a moment and take dithyrambic flight.

Dieudonné Labalbarie was—dare I say it—even more admirable than his father. Conceived at a glorious hour of triumph over haughty rivals, he embodied the ideal of robust virtue as fully as the most serious of credit institutions can reckon.

At fifteen, he had already invested his savings, and he kept his person as tidy as his books. If one audited his record, nothing frivolous could be found.

It would have been the height of injustice to fault him for a single minute of transport—a fit, even repressed, of mad pity for anyone about anything.

His lucky father had to grab the till or counter to keep his balance when speaking of him—so drunk did it make him to have sired such a boy.

This child of benediction still lives and thrives. Indeed, he has even doubled his patrimony in the three years he has been an orphan, having succeeded in making himself dear to a woman who owes her extreme wealth to tortoise farming. He has just married her, and many people would no doubt recognize him if I did not fear offending the lily of his modesty by endeavoring to sketch his amiable likeness.

Whoever can do so may guess. I am saying too much, perhaps, in affirming that he possesses the physiognomy of a handsome reptile and is ordinarily accompanied by a mastiff of utterly monstrous dimensions.

Hear now the infinitely little-known tale of the father's death and obsequies. Amateurs of dulcet emotion are welcome to read no further.

One morning, the coroner determined that the great Fiacre had ceased to exist.

Labalbarie *fils* immediately went to work. Without wasting vain tears or otherwise squandering the precious "stuff" of his own life—that is, time (in the noble words of Benjamin Franklin, whom he quoted incessantly)—he put everything in order and made preparations without losing so much as a moment.

At 10:35, newspapers were informed that he was in mourning. In thousandfold copy, expression of his grief blew in every direction—on all the winds of the compass-rose. The letters of notice had been judiciously ordered and printed in advance.

The same was true of the plaque of black marble destined for the columbarium. It displayed a phoenix spreading its wings amid flames, and it bore the terrifying inscription that the deceased had requested:

I WILL BE REBORN

The son then completed a bicycle ride to renew his fibers in the vivifying air, enjoyed a copious meal, received a few tearful visitors, went to perform his devotions at the Stock Exchange, effected a few profitable collections toward eventide, and spent the night on the town so as to punctuate the extreme violence of his chagrin.

The following day, a sumptuous hearse bedecked with flowers, attended by a throng little inclined to contemplation, brought the remains of the deceased to the Crematory.

"Ah! Ah! You will be reborn!" the genial Dieudonné said to himself, in the fearsome *chambre ardente*, where two men charged with putting his father in the oven had accompanied him. "We'll just see if you're reborn!..."

The coffin—fashioned out of light boards according to administrative regulation (so that an atmosphere of seven hundred degrees would consume it promptly)—rested on a mechanical trolley with two metal projections; when given a vigorous push, said equipment plunges the dead into the furnace and recoils with a screech: a diastolic and systolic movement that is completed in twenty-five seconds.

That's where Dieudonné stood—in filial meditation—*when a noise was heard within the coffin . . .*

Oh! It was a muffled and altogether vague sound, I assure you, but a sound all the same—like a man mistaken for dead trying to move in his shroud. It even seemed that the coffin shook . . .

At that very instant, the door of the oven, expertly operated, flung wide open.

Three faces reddened by the horrible flame exchanged glances.

"The body's just emptying," Dieudonné calmly declared.

All the same, the other two hesitated.

"Well, come on! Hell and Damnation!" the parricide shouted suddenly. "I'm telling you: it's just the body emptying." And he planted a stack of bills in the hand of the man standing at his side.

The metal shafts leapt forward and shot back.

Then the door closed—but no doubt not fast enough, for Dieudonné, who had made sure to stand right in front, thought he detected, in the instant it took the coffin to burn, his father's hands stretching toward him and a face disfigured by despair.

XV.   The End of Don Juan

> It's nice to talk with a man
> Who only has one head.
>
> JULES VALLÈS

"And the wretch died as he lived—exulting in riches. It wasn't even that he had been a spendthrift, a wastrel. In all the world, he was the first, people said, to place his capital to full advantage. Anyway, he died without the slightest infirmity and in full self-possession—even though he was very old, like a patriarch from before the Flood. It seems a bit much. Without strictly demanding—like a schoolboy nursed on the milk of kindly fathers—that 'the finger of God' intervene, one should have wished, for Justice's sake, that the miscreant's final agony hadn't been so gentle."

Thus spoke, without any malice, a man offended by the insolent glory of the Marquis de la Tour de Pise.

This entirely too-well-known personage had barely breathed his last. For many years, one thought him eternal. He had been born in Merrie Olde England when the emigration started—when Louis XVI still had a head on his shoulders; public rumor affirmed that he enjoyed full vigor even as he approached his ninetieth year. The marvel was little verified, no doubt, yet it was accredited by several enthusiastic disciples who had passed the age of sixty themselves and now feared the cold.

The fact of the matter is that Marquis Hector de la Tour de Pise cast rays like a monstrance. It was accepted without question that, once upon a time, queens had pined for love "as they entered his chamber," and that a tribe of Ariadnes sobbed on his account.

Long before the celebrated Beauvivier came to console us, he excelled at introducing his person in adjudications and even in *actions*. Hence his opulence. Up until the final days, one saw even the haughtiest families paying a dear price for the *relics* of his alcove . . .

Such, at any rate, was the universally accepted legend concerning this heartbreaker. The buttons from his undergarments, mounted as pendants, are considered inestimable jewels at the present hour.

"—But my dear sir," the midwife replied, "you've got it all wrong. I wasn't there for the villain's death, but I can assure you that Ixion was never more cruelly punished. Imagine whatever you like, but you'll never appreciate the extent of the horror. Rest upon this fetus extending you its arms, and lend me your ear. I'm in the mood for storytelling this morning."

"Marquis Hector was a handsome man, it's true, and he appeared to be the consummate *grand seigneur*. Envious parties never could deny it. He differed from the crowd so markedly that as soon as he made an entrance, *everyone seemed to look the same.*

"He could have made the public pay to see him, like a true monster. Instead, he made do with audiences in private—and in exchange for sizeable sums, which he devoted to enterprises of the most solid kind; his flair for speculation when faced with the worst of complications is well known.

"But that is of middling interest. In an age when all men are, almost without exception, streetwalkers, this gentleman's whoredom and the financial aptitudes that attended it are nothing unheard of. They go together so well.

"I can share something much better—and I've promised you horrors difficult to conceive, haven't I? If your thirst for his atonement is not slaked after my tale, it's because nothing could ever quench it.

"To begin with, do you even know what he had to atone for? No. Like everyone else, you think only of the more or less odious existence of a vampire wholly absorbed by acts of turpitude for almost a century, which he drifted down as if on a brook of putrefaction, never even glancing at the faces of those who toil and suffer. That point of view is as banal as common prayer, my good sir. In fact, the matter is something immeasurably subtler.

"You shall do me the honor, I hope, of believing I don't give a damn about trade secrets—like any other midwife (of a higher calling, of course). That's for doctors, who most of the time have no other way of avoiding the galleys.

"Well, then! I had the handsome Hector as a customer. He was married two times, and he killed at least one of his wives without my assistance. He operated perfectly on his own and enlisted the aid of no one.

"I delivered his first child without further thought—then his second, ten years later, toward the end of the reign of Louis-Philippe, just as I would have done for a servant or working girl. Both times, the marquis had insisted on being alone with me.

"The first time, we delivered a kind of satyr without eyes or mouth; instead of a nose, it had a kind of flabby and pendulous membrane I will not describe, as you are a sensitive man . . . With blood as cold as the dead, La Tour de Pise took hold of the runt before I could stop him and gave it to the mother to kiss; she died two hours later.

"The second child of the marquis had two heads on a spindly body—more or less without arms or legs. It was another print of *the same image*.

"This time, the mother wasn't allowed to see it. I rolled the little abomination into my apron and darted out of the room. That's how I lost the noble seigneur's custom, but I had guessed many things; later, I learned still more . . ."

"You are now convinced," the terrible matron continued, lowering her voice in a strange manner, "that I have been speaking of Crime and Punishment. Behold, the bronze fiber of your implacable justice is already going slack— like a guitar loosening its strings after thirty dogs have pissed on it. Well, you're farther off than ever, you hear?

"Our profession stands right at the edge of the sewer; one sees things emerge that make it difficult for one to be surprised over time. And yet, monsieur, the man in question astounded me—and he still astounds me, to the point of terror.

"Had it only been what you just heard, this man would not be more than another horrid miscreant in the vast mass of lowlifes we encounter, and he would scarcely deserve to be mentioned. But let me tell you again, that's not how it is. His punishment will make you tremble, if you can understand it.

"Did you notice the strange *identity* between the monstrous phenomena, repeated over ten years and with two legitimate spouses (both of whom he married for money, needless to say)? I am convinced that further trial would have yielded the same results.

"To speak plainly, the marquis was an IDOLATER—a fervent and thoroughgoing idolater; inwardly shaped to resemble his god, he could not but reproduce its likeness *outwardly* when he attempted to procreate.

"By himself, he venerated—in a shrine mysteriously lighted—that part of his body that the priests of Cybele once held in such great honor. *He had cast a mold of himself,* fashioned an object with the aid of an exceptionally able workman. Displayed in a kind of tabernacle, it received, every day, the obsecrations of this Corybant—whom polite society considered a high roller (just as the small fry of boarding schools have swallowed the lie that the Buddhist Charcot was a doctor). We will never know the number of people who are other than what they seem to their peers.

"That, monsieur, was his true crime—the most egregious of attacks in the eyes of those who know and have peered into the depths. Everything else flowed from it.

"Now hear the expiation that lasted ten years, until the eve of his death.

"Every night, without fail, a most imposing and handsome old man— one whom the proudest women had loved and all tramps now know—huddled in the shadows, at the last hour of trade.

"His tastes were well known. The exchange would proceed: as filthy as possible on the woman's part, and altogether humble on his—for he insisted on playing the role of a nasty customer consumed by unutterable wishes.

"Naturally, after a few minutes—which he measured to the second with a timepiece—agreement was reached.

"Then the woman, leaning against the wall, would offer him first one foot, then the other, each in turn; sprawling on the ground—rain or shine— the octogenarian, groaning in ecstasy, would lick *the soles of her boots*.

"Such was the final demand of the little deity of the conqueror— whom three generations of imbeciles have compared to Don Juan."

XVI.   A Martyr

"And so, my worthy son-in-law, it would seem even religious considerations cannot sway your soul. You won't even wait until tomorrow to *indulge your filthiness*, I can see. You take no pity on this poor child, raised to this very day with the purity of an angel, whom you will defile with your reptile's breath. Well then, by God! May your will be done and your holy name be blessed for ever and ever!"

"Amen," replied Georges, lighting a cigar. "For the last time, dear mother-in-law, you may be certain of my eternal gratitude. I thank you for your prayers, infinitely; nor shall I, believe you me, forget your urgings. Good evening."

The train began to move. Madame Durable, standing on the platform, watched the express fly away, carrying the newlyweds south.

Still raging with the day's stormy sentiments, but with eyes as dry as enamel exiting a kiln, she nervously tapped the ground with the point of her umbrella.

Angrily calculating her sacrifices and holocausts, the dear soul told herself that it had been hard, well and truly hard, to have lived for twenty years only for the sake of an ungrateful daughter who was now abandoning her like this—just as soon as she had wed—to follow a stranger clearly devoid of modesty who would profane her, no doubt, with his shameless caresses almost immediately.

"Ah! But yes, to be sure, that's the thanks one gets from one's children! Just think, monsieur," she said—almost unconsciously addressing the ju-

nior stationmaster, who had come to induce her, in civil terms, to go away—
"Just think! We bring them into the world under appalling pain you cannot
even begin to imagine, we raise them in fear of the good Lord, and we try
to make them like angels that they may be worthy to sing forever at the feet
of the Lamb. One prays for them ceaselessly—day and night, for a third of
one's life. For the good of these tender souls, one does penance; the thought
alone makes me shudder! And look how they repay you! Just look at her!
She abandons me—casts me away like a rag, like a potato peel—just as soon
as some degenerate shows up. I was foolish enough to welcome him, because he seemed like a good Christian; right away, he took full advantage of
the chance to soil an innocent heart, to present impure visions to her, and
to make a young person raised in the holiest ignorance believe—dare I say
it—that the filthy caresses of a spouse of flesh and blood might give her
fuller joy than a mother's chaste effusions of tenderness . . .

"And you see what happens, monsieur. May you testify as much on the
Day of Judgment! I have been left—abandoned, betrayed, and alone in the
world—without consolation or hope. Put yourself in my place."

"Madame," the employee responded, "I beg you to believe that I sym-
pathize with your chagrin. It is my duty, however, to observe that the exi-
gencies of my service will not permit me to let you stand here any longer. I
implore you, therefore, and to my own great regret, kindly to depart."

Dismissed in this fashion, the afflicted mother then vanished—but
not without calling upon the heavens, one last time, to witness the immen-
sity of her sorrow.

Madame Virginie Durable, née Mucus, embodied the insufficiently admired type of the *martyr*.

Indeed, she was a martyr of Lyons—and consequently, the most horrid little vixen one can conceive.

From childhood on, she had delivered herself to the cruelest of butchers, never knowing the refreshment of humane consolation. The universe,
incidentally, had been regularly informed of her torments.

Thirty years earlier, when Monsieur Durable—who is today a retired oystermonger—had married this burnt offering, the poor man had hardly suspected that he was taking on the terrible office of torturer.

He promptly learned as much; in the course of time, it deprived him of his wits entirely.

Whatever he said or did, he never—not even once—managed not to be criminal, not to trample upon his wife's heart, nor to plant daggers and thorns in it.

Virginie was one of those kindly creatures who have "suffered so much"—a woman no man deserves, whom no one can understand or console, and who has not arms enough to petition the heavens.

She wore—it goes without saying—a sublime piety it would be ridiculous to pretend one admired sufficiently; indeed, it never ceased to amaze even her.

In a word, she was a spouse who stood beyond reproach—Ah! Good God!—one who unfailingly brought the rarest of benedictions upon the commercial enterprise of a no-good dunce who couldn't appreciate his good fortune.

One day, a few years after they had wed, the martyr was still young and appetizing enough, it seems. The odious personage surprised her while she was in the company of an underdressed gentleman.

The circumstances were such that one would have had to be not only blind, but as deaf as death itself to harbor the slightest doubt.

The austerely devout woman cuckolding him with an eagerness that was clearly shared did not have enough literary culture to offer him the words of Ninon, but her words were almost as eloquent.

She marched upon him, breasts bared; in a most dulcet tone—a voice profoundly earnest and sweet—she said to the stupefied man:

"My dear, I am doing business with Monsieur the Count. So go about your own affairs, won't you?" After that, she closed the door.

And it was finished. Two hours later, she indicated to her husband that she no longer had a word to say to him, barring cases of absolute emergency, and declared that she was tired of lowering herself to the level of a shopkeeper; indeed, she was to be pitied for having sacrificed her maidenly hopes to a boor without ideals, who moreover had the indelicacy to spy on her.

As she was the daughter of a bailiff, she also did not fail to recall the superiority of her birth on the occasion.

From this day forth, this Christian of the first centuries bore a palm branch wheresoever she stepped. Life became a hell—a lake of abyssal bitterness for the poor, domesticated cuckold; he began to drink, and he grew sufficiently idiotic to be plausibly and charitably consigned to an asylum.

By extraordinary luck, Mademoiselle Durable's education was better than circumstances might have suggested.

It is true that her virtuous mother—who applied herself without respite to the stupefaction of Monsieur Durable and, what is more, to pursuing obscure farces—bothered very little with her. Early on, she abandoned the girl to the mercenary vigilance of the sisters of the Stairs of Pilate—who, miraculously, acquitted themselves of their duties in a conscientious fashion.

Supplied with a reasonable dowry and fit to be seen in every respect, the young girl zealously seized the first opportunity to get married that came along—just as soon as she had penetrated the ridiculousness and the execrable malice of the old bitch (who promptly, and by the mysterious decree of dreaded Providence, turned into a *mother-in-law*).

The bravery of the groom was generally admired.

The ceremony was barely concluded when the latter, possessing quite the independent mind, declared his resolute intention to remove himself immediately—along with his wife—via express train. All present had been able to see that the decision, which was no doubt reached in joint consultation, did not pain the young bride in the least; indeed, she seemed to accord slight notice to maternal wails and reproaches.

Madame Durable, raging with indignation of the most generous kind, had then returned to her lonesome house, meditating hellish vengeance.

But no . . . "Vengeance" isn't the right word. It was a matter of punishment.

This outraged mother had the right to punish. In fact, she had the obligation—so that the Fourth Commandment of Divine Law might remain in vigor.

From then on, any and all means were legitimate; pious intention would perfume the most venomous of schemes.

In executing her commendable designs, the martyr was henceforth attentive to procuring, by all the little games and tricks she could contrive, the dishonor of her son-in-law and the dishonor of her daughter.

The former was accused of monstrous vices—unspeakable habits that appalling witnesses had certified. The young woman received letters that could have been sent from Sodom.

Madame Breech wrote various grievances, and a certain Tom Thumb advised her that "it wouldn't do to carry on like this." A torrent of obscenities inundated the newlyweds' nuptial bed.

For his part, the husband was assaulted by a countless array of anonymous or pseudonymous messages that varied in style but were always unctuous and dripping with the most genial commiseration, cautioning him about the unclean past of his companion: her breath alone had putrefied fifty young girls in the dormitories at school, and she certainly couldn't have offered him, *with her dowry*, anything but base and vestigial bodily virginity.

No words can describe the diabolical malice—the infernal skill pulling at the strings of imposturous intrigue—that seasoned horrid poisons of infanticide every day.

It lasted more than six months. Soon the unfortunate couple, who initially felt nothing but profound scorn, were seized by the horror of abiding persecution.

They learned that letters—all of which came from the same *unknown* source—had been sent to the hotels where they stayed, both to the proprietors and to the staff; they even rained on notables of the cities and villages they traversed in their flight.

They found themselves in the clutches of panicked, continual anguish—mauled beyond repair by suspicions they knew to be absurd but could do nothing about. Finally, they sank into a cesspool of melancholy.

They no longer slept. They no longer ate. Their souls extravasated into pale pits where hope is washed away into nonexistence.

Finally, one day, they died together—at the same hour and at the same place—and no one could determine with any precision just how their sufferings had ceased.

The mother who had followed them like a shark ensured that suicide was registered as the cause of death—so the couple would be excluded from Christian burial grounds.

She is—more and more—the Martyr. Every day, she ascends to the third heaven with the greatest of ease, and at the final hour of every evening—according to the chronicle of the Rue de Constantinople—she rings for a hearty *valet de chambre*.

XVII. Suspicion

The number of imbeciles may well be infinite, as the canonical expression in Ecclesiastes holds, yet it would be difficult to encounter or conceive of an idiot as perfect as the merchant of moth repellant whose noisy suicide all the newspapers have been reporting (or might have been reporting) for the last few days.

As far as the history of famous cretins goes, there's nothing more to be said once Aristobolus is mentioned. (May leave be given that we conceal our hero's patronymic with this transparent anagram.)

Aristobolus was born—to the great astonishment of many—at the age of fifty-five. That is to say, from his first feeding bottle on, he displayed such caution as is ordinarily reserved for citizens who have achieved majority three times over.

Still in swaddling clothes, the good-natured child already defied the whole world. Whether taciturn out of circumspection or bawling in calculation, he drooled suspicion until the day his bond of dentition fell due.

His parents thought that heaven had showered them with blessings for having engendered such a son; before he could even speak, he supervised the servants, had himself lifted up onto chairs to verify the contents of the larder, and would not consent to sleep until he had peered underneath all the beds.

A sneak and an informer as a schoolboy, he made himself hated among his peers for his weaselly ways and the hermetic silence in which his empty, villainous heart sealed itself up.

The only thought he seemed capable of excogitating at the time—and subsequently, too, until the end of his miserable days—was that the entire world practiced dissimulation with the same sustained and prodigious attention that he did; that those who were most expansive and who talked the most were precisely the ones to watch out for.

When the dirty orchard of concupiscence began to blossom, around his seventeenth spring, he did not take a virtuous stand against the tempter-goat; instead, he did his best to disappoint the Adversary each time the horn pointed at him—so that he would not fall victim to the heinous treachery of women.

Well then, from the outset this full-bodied imbecile had something that offered the illusion of depth. He was a bastard of the shadows, as Hugo would have said—a fetus of opacity, it seemed, always floating in a jar of darkness.

But one day, he married. There's no denying that business is business. Attention to the commercial prosperity of "Aristobolus and Son" imperiously demanded that a fitting heiress mount his bed, which, until now, had ignored all debauchery.

Likely, it will never be known what offices were performed in this mysterious place of rest. However, a number of particularities—gathered with scrupulous precision—suggest that the couple's molecules combined a little less frequently than the cycle of equinoxes.

This mode of conjugality did not keep Aristobolus from being consumed by a wild boar's jealousy; the laudable effect was that his ass of a wife learned a thing or two—immeasurably better and faster than would have occurred by way of even the most skillful and winning tenderness.

However great my ambition to be disagreeable may be, I wouldn't dare affirm that her lovers numbered as many as the stars. That said, I imagine that if one brought them all together on a vast plain, it would yield a host excellently suited to the solemn manifestation of impassioned patriotism.

No doubt the unfortunate industrialist detected, or thought he had detected, a goodly number of stories. But he was stuck in the axis of such a furious whirlwind that he could never focus his rage on a determinate point: his wife's consolers might be likened to the invisible rays of a cartwheel rolling by at blinding speed.

He even came to doubt Arithmetic! Incertitude and suspicion gripped the poor cuckold firmly, and each day his intelligence grew dimmer and dimmer. He descended to the bottom floor, where atheists of the Number rot away. Suddenly, he had ceased to credit the probity of figures . . .

On that day of enormous tribulation, at the hour of black distress and infinite dereliction, a selfless friend—perhaps the only one his wife would have rejected—came and advised him that a drop in moth-oil stock would effect his ruin if he did not take vigorous measures without delay.

Aristobolus, it should now be abundantly plain, distrusted everything under the heavens. In this regard, his intransigence was absolute. Suspicion was the principle of his life, the Twelve Tablets of his Law, and his supreme credo. He could have been its martyr.

What am I saying? Hadn't he been just that for forty years? In his line—to be sure, one of the most estimable in all our civilization, where mutual good faith stands most rigorously inviolate—the perpetual fear of pits and snares had, quite literally, harassed, flagellated, tortured, skinned, trepanated, fumigated, wrenched, drawn, and quartered him, every evening and every morning.

He had fallen out with a host of affable correspondents whose patience matched the patriarch's very own. He had bungled royal affairs that would have enriched him beyond measure.

In his house of commerce, filled with turmoil and rushing confusion, the sales clerks came and went in single file; not a one of them proved able to discover the brilliant platitude that might have permitted him to shut down, even for twenty-four hours, the locomoting machinery. By some miracle, he escaped bankruptcy.

And so, one can just imagine the mien with which he received the rash friend who had been moved to pity (however implausibly) at the prospect of the brute's imminent undoing.

On the spot, Aristobolus made his judgment known. He declared his friend a horrible rogue—a filthy traitor who was setting a hellish trap for him. As a result, he did precisely the opposite of what had been recommended. A few weeks later, he was obliged to cut his losses.

But this wreck cast a beam into his night. He clearly saw, or thought he saw clearly, that he had not been deceived. For the first time, he thought it right for his wife to call him a sucker, a good-for-nothing, and even—in a flagrant contradiction of terms—a *panderer* (for such was his partner's first impulse).

All the same, he was still afraid of being tricked.

"Why," he asked the prophet (seemingly from the depths of a cave), "Why warn me, then?"

The other man simply explained that he had been concerned lest poverty befall the couple (even though Madame Aristobolus had never deigned to grant him the slightest notice).

These words of truth—should I have leave to borrow the reverent style of Holy Writ on such an occasion—revived, in the merchant's ransacked soul, the youthful vigor of *meleagris meleagris* (an animal described by Aristotle, now held to be the turkey).

"The creep's talking about my wife!" he yelled. "There must be something going on."

Without delay, he called her to account and cruelly accused her of having slept with the double-crosser.

However, Madame Aristobolus had long since arrived at diabolical insight into her husband's suspicious nature. She fired back a response that hit him with the accuracy of the discus cast by the discobolus:

"Yes, my dear, you're a cuckold."

This, without question, was an affirmation. Therefore, according to his system, it represented an act of imposture. Now, fraud seemed to stand all around him, at every side. He crawled deep into his demented cretinism and, despairing that he was not *unquestionably* a cuckold, did away with himself.

XVIII.   The Telephone of Calypso

Madame Presque was disconsolate about Monsieur Vertige's departure. In the six months since a profoundly equitable decree pronouncing their divorce had set an end to their conjugal tribulations, the exquisite woman had little by little let herself succumb to melancholy.

The initial transports of a joy altogether natural had promptly been followed by spells of solitude, alarms of insomnia, fires of continence, and, finally, bitter regrets.

The reason for this, however, was not that Monsieur Vertige was exactly loveable. Ah! God, no. He smelled like a goat, had a vicious personality, and possessed not so much as a globule of enthusiasm for his wife.

Yet there was a certain savor to him—that special something which makes one always return to such brutes. It's inexplicable, no doubt, but all too certain.

She could claim in all fairness that, prior to the divorce, she had done everything a good woman can do to grow sick of her husband. She had even thought she might guarantee success. She had taken several lovers of uncommon distinction. Above all, there had been the first; indeed, it can be said with certainty that he, a high-ranking official in the administration of the Catacombs, incarnated her ideal type.

Well, then! These auspicious attempts and the favorable divorce that resulted had not managed to separate her from her husband entirely. She could not help thinking of the unappetizing man.

No doubt, she didn't go so far as to regret that she was no longer Madame Vertige, but it became clearer and clearer that her banished spouse had provided the indispensable condiment to her joys. In other words, love was insipid now that she was no longer cuckolding a legitimate license-holder.

One would have to be the lowest of all men not to appreciate, not to feel, the extent to which divorce exalts the heart. At the same time, one must recognize that it is not exactly a lending institution. To employ her own, familiar expression, Madame Presque found her affairs in a state of embarrassment.

The money had vanished at the same time as Monsieur Vertige. It had disappeared down a hole, so to speak. To thoughtful eyes, the circumstance certainly counted for something in the melancholy experienced by the abandoned woman.

Her amorous enterprises had not proven profitable. Far from it. In fear (which was truly puerile) lest she seem to be prostituting herself, she had experienced the admirable ease with which gentlemen tolerate being unburdened of importunate service charges; the inconstant and ungrateful parties she had formerly regaled would scarcely come running to assist her now. No crowds formed outside the furnished room (tenth class) that had taken the place of yesteryear's comfortable accommodations; the matter of quotidian subsistence began to weigh heavy.

At the height of such anxiety, a refreshing idea wafted down on her—like a breeze of perfume in the desert.

She recalled the telephone that Monsieur Vertige owned. Often, the apparatus had woken her during the night (this was but one of her innumerable grievances).

She had revenged herself by making the irresponsible vehicle of modern turpitude and folly serve various plans of her own. On sufficiently many occasions, Monsieur Vertige had been informed of nugatory meetings that compelled him to absent himself for hours—and from them, his wife had boldly profited. At the office, he must have been considered a veritable workhorse. The kidding had gone so far that there was reason to fear he might decide simply not to pick up at all.

Meditating a mysterious design, Madame Presque dashed to the next telephone booth and asked to be connected.

At this juncture, allow me to include a parenthetical remark (one that is altogether useless, I hasten to add) and declare that the telephone is one of my hatreds.

It is immoral, I maintain, for people to speak to each other from so far away, and the aforementioned device is a hellish contraption.

Needless to say, I can provide no positive proof that this *voice-elongator* has a tenebrous origin; I am unable to document my affirmation. I must simply appeal to parties of good faith and firm character who have used it.

The ghostly rustling prior to conversation—does it not warn of passage into sealed chambers perhaps overflowing with horror . . . if only one knew?

Then, there's the horrible disfigurement of human sounds. One would think a rolling mill had flattened them out, and it seems they reach the ear only by distending themselves monstrously. Isn't there something frightful about this, too?

A few days ago, an old bachelor of the scientific bathhouses—who receives bonuses specifically for coaxing out *useful* discoveries at the hammam of a mighty journalistic organ—hymned the glories of an English factory that had just exterminated Scripture.

It seems that a radiant machine will replace the hand of mortals, who will no longer need to write at all. Naturally, this puppet encouraged the peoples of the Earth to rejoice at such progress.

I consider the telephone to pose a more serious threat: it debases the Word itself.

"Hello! Hello! With whom do I have the honor of speaking?"

"It's me, Charlotte, your former wife."

"Ah! Very well, dear Madame, how are you getting on?"

"Not bad, thank you. And yourself?"

"Oh my, I'm gaining weight! How may I be of service, if you please?"

"Grant me a rendezvous as soon as possible for an altogether urgent matter."

"Pardon, Madame, I have the honor of reminding you that we are no longer supposed to see each other."

"Ah, very well, my dear Ferdinand, my little snookums; that must change. What good is being divorced if we can no longer see each other?"

"What do you mean? Please explain yourself," responded the ex-spouse. It seemed the *extremity* of his reproachful voice protruded from the receiver—upon which Madame Presque planted a kiss, which the apparatus transmitted like a sting.

"Pay attention, ducky, and do try to understand what I'm saying. When we got married, we acted like children; we've almost missed out on life because we understood nothing—truly, nothing at all—of what nature required of us.

"Free love, that's what we needed. Marriage is for inferior beings, and we were called for a higher life. We'd have been perfectly happy if we'd have been smart enough not to get married and not to stupidly live under the same roof; we should just have seen each other every now and then, like two little pigs in love.

"Why not make this beautiful dream a reality? Do you really think it's too late? Listen to me, you naughty boy, and see if I love you:

"I'LL CHEAT ON THE WHOLE WORLD WITH YOU! My Ferdinand . . ."

It's likely Madame Presque already knew the spiritual manure this promise would land in, for the two segments of the serpent of adultery, severed by divorce and rejoined by squalid infidelity, formed a more perfect union.

XIX.   A Recruit

The poor devil compared himself to the fox—the poor devil of a fox he had surprised one day, at least ten or fifteen years ago, in the middle of the woods.

It was deepest winter. Long fasting had emaciated the limping animal; with hardly enough strength to drag even its own weight, it carried in its mouth a skinny hare, which starvation had also chased out of its burrow. Catching it must have cost hours of pain, lying in wait, for this father of kits; no doubt they were awaiting his return impatiently.

When it noticed the walker, the unfortunate *vermin* had tried to flee over the snow. But it seems it was thoroughly exhausted, for it was forced to stop almost right away lest it drop its prey; the man, who had already raised his stick, suddenly lacked the power to strike such a miserable being.

And so he had simply gone his way. He was satisfied with the clemency he had shown, but he held onto the memory of the suffering beast's eyes, which had transfixed him with a most intelligent look of despair.

He thought he had detected in this stare, in addition to the rage of a wild animal in dire straits, something resembling human pain. He didn't forget it and called it to mind on more than one occasion, experiencing anguish of his own. Then, cruelly, that same look became clearer than ever.

"I felt pity for the creature," he groaned. "Why am I not pitied myself?"

He, too, was expected at his den. Over the many hours since he had left his ailing wife and three little children, he had had plenty of time to die of cold and hunger. (Needless to say, the kindly landlord must have taken advantage of his absence to heap further insults upon them.)

What to do? My God! What to do? He had climbed up and down a thousand steps. He had spoken, prayed, supplicated, and sobbed—without getting a thing. Faint with exhaustion, he could hardly even walk; he started to envy the old fox, which had at least held something in its mouth . . .

He had just left a very wealthy individual who, he believed, might prove accommodating; once, he had had the opportunity to offer one of those services it is not easy to forget. Yet his fellow man, radiant with ingratitude, spoke of his own setbacks: a gigantic undertaking that had cost him several million in lost profit. Then, he gently led him back to the stairs and fed him a line about how he should work with his own two hands.

A few hours earlier, a party of exalted piety had gravely regretted, as he stood before him, the abominable cant of hypocritical philanthropists and windbag sociologists. At the end of the interview, he bestowed the precious advice that he should place his trust in God.

This man of goodwill, who was always ready to sacrifice himself, had not hesitated to forfeit the delight of conversation with his many dinner guests so that he might offer the indigent friar his exhortations; thereby, he had seen to it that a *single* cup of excellent coffee was served—a good third of which he shared with his faithful dog.

And so it went everywhere else, too. Finally, the rain itself declared its hostility toward the desperate man—piercing black rain that soaked him to his very heart. He thought himself trapped in a kennel of demons. At that instant, he was judged fit to collaborate in the world's salvation.

Two steps away, taking shelter beneath the same coach gate, a stranger was observing him keenly.

This man was unknown, yet wanted by police forces throughout Europe. He had one of those faces made of putty—the kind it seems one might use to falsify a key for even the most complicated lock, the kind in which a fortuneteller would detect the *life line* of the party causing one's affliction. It was one of those modifiable and impersonal faces that seem to serve no purpose other than to reflect the sallow fear of the teeming masses.

He cut a pathetic figure. A single blow from a feeble arm could cut him down—anyone's heel might trample upon him—and even the alertest compassion would not stir; the simple idea of misfortune or prejudice would not be roused. That's how removed he seemed from all sublunary solidarity.

He was one of those Beings begotten of Silent Wrath that have just enough human surface to embody the Social Danger of which they provide the fearsome likeness.

They are strange packages tossed this way and that in express trains and transatlantic shipping vessels, which make their presence felt at the precise instant the spark of Universal Disquiet springs forth from the heart of the afflicted and dying.

Repressive measures can do nothing against them. They are colorless and dilute, like the gloaming at dusk. A ghost always intervenes just when the arm of the law thinks they can be seized.

Surging suddenly, Death obeys these absences—like the dog of a nighttime thief, and Terror strides before them in velvet boots . . .

And so, the dreadful stranger watched the man dying of hunger; his single eye, fringed with pale lashes, resembled a silver-colored spider at the center of its web.

"Hey! It's funny, isn't it?" he said suddenly. "It's really funny to ask for a crumb from upstanding citizens when you're dying of hunger, when your children are crying and the sky is pissing everywhere."

Hearing this faithful echo of his inner grievances, the wanderer could not keep from exhaling his lamentation.

"Ah! The pigs . . . " he sighed.

Then, all of a sudden he thought better:

"So you know me, Monsieur?"

"I don't know a soul," the other responded. "If anyone claims to know me, he's tucked away where he'll never get out. All it takes is just a look at you, my poor, good sir. Your face is like a straw mattress they've all cleaned their boots on. You haven't eaten for two days—I can see the way you drag your paws. The corner of your eye has the twitch of a poor sod who isn't suffering just for his own carcass, either. Come on, you deadbeat, take a look at the paperwork. A hundred twenty thousand in small change for a room with a garden and a comfortable chamber pot. Just a crust of bread! Well, then! You look like you're up for auction. I can read you as quick as you'd eat a roast chicken. Come on, how much for your hide? I'll buy it."

"Monsieur," the half-starved man said in turn, "you're wrong to make fun of me. I assure you I'm in no mood for jokes."

The stranger smiled; his bare, black teeth made him seem even paler.

"It's true," he said, "I've got a sense of humor. I've pulled some pretty good ones that even got a few laughs. I'm actually *in demand* for that. But it's not always fun and games. Listen to me well, and try not to make me repeat myself. I don't usually talk for this long. Here's a hundred-franc note. Go eat your fill, stuff your family—make them burst if you can—have a good time, then come find me tomorrow. 366 Rue Ramey, at old Papa Bissextil's. *Ask for Monsieur* RENARD. Got it? Goodnight."

One must assume this high roller possessed a rare gift of penetration, and that he knew perfectly well what he was doing, for the following evening, the two men left for Barcelona, where, no doubt, a matter of great urgency had summoned them.

XX.   Botched Sacrilege

On the afternoon of that holy day, the peasant women who were huddled here and there around the confessional suddenly—and with the most respectful haste—scattered to make way for the Viscountess Brunissende des Egards as she approached the Tribunal of Penitence in all her finery.

The confessor was a simple, good-natured fellow, a missionary of the Congregation of Lazarists. He had been sent to preach Lent here in the countryside, where people were still religious, and to give a hand to the old parish priest during Easter ablutions.

The radiant Viscountess who reigned over the land—the very archetype of magnificence for the poor in her fiefdom—came and kneeled, rapidly and without shilly-shallying, within the modest compartment appointed for the sacrament of reconciliation.

The missionary took notice and hastened to absolve a clogmaker who clung to him in the other chamber; almost as quickly, he opened the floodgate of exhortations to the notable penitent whom the heavens had sent him.

She didn't let him get a word in edgewise.

"Monsieur clergyman," she said right away, "I imagine your time is precious, and let me tell you that I myself have but a few moments to spare. My seventeenth lover impatiently awaits me—an adorable dunce to whom I have resolved to surrender body and soul in an hour or two.

"I'm as much an atheist as one can be, and I do whatever I like. I loathe the poor, I hate pain, and I prefer a bad conscience to a bad tooth—as a Jewish poet you wouldn't know put it so well.

"I scorn your bloody God, and I don't want to have anything to do with the absolution you dispense to the good people of this village. However, my husband is a virtuous deputy, and he needs his electors to admire him. What would they say in these parts if they found out that the Viscountess des Egards doesn't take communion?

"No, no. One is obliged to preach by example. I hereby declare I will have the pleasure of receiving the bread of angels from your hand Sunday next, at high mass.

"Now, Father, I imagine the time of an ordinary confession has elapsed; the pious souls surrounding us should be sufficiently edified by my Christian sentiments, and it would be inexcusable for me to monopolize your ministry. Thus, I shall withdraw modestly, as befits a sinner who has just been reconciled with her Savior. I request the honor of your presence, as soon as possible, at the chateau; there I shall most humbly endeavor to return the favor of the Holy Table that you have rendered."

A moment later, the lady of the manor had prosternated herself at the foot of the altar (no doubt to utter a word of devotion) and exited the church as a frigate leaves the harbor; behind her trailed a wake of strange perfumes the women of the village breathed in like the spices of Paradise.

The next day, as soon as he had delivered mass, the clergyman ascended to Chateau Egards and had his presence announced to Brunissende.

The right-minded servants admired him as a man of the cloth of uncustomary length—some kind of sacerdotal phenicopter one might think fashioned especially for finding lost sheep, or drachmas minted long ago, which can be difficult to locate beneath the sumptuous furnishings of rich dwellings where disorder has made a home.

His countenance indicated sixty years—as water levels mark the great harvests of a river—and on this occasion his physiognomy offered the spectacle of a kindly ruminant routed and harassed by inexpressible torments.

He was introduced, but he had to wait for more than an hour. As everyone knows, the first duty of preachers today is to wait for beautiful ladies to rise when they have the leisure, or otherwise deign to receive them.

"Ah! My dear Father," said the Viscountess when she finally condescended to make her appearance, "What a lovely surprise! I rushed from bed to receive you, but truly I fear I have made you wait—despite myself, I swear. I count on your charity to excuse a woman of the world who could not possibly have guessed that you would do her the honor of wishing her good morning so early."

"Madame, the sun rose five hours ago; already many millions of Christians have suffered. A great number agonize and despair even now . . . " the missionary replied, rather curtly. "I would not have come and bothered you so early—nor even later, you may believe—if the honor of God had not made it my urgent duty . . . .

"I owe you a cruel night, Madame. This morning, it seemed that a terrible angel was dragging me to your doorstep by the hair. I have come to ask if you are ready to die."

The pretty woman erupted in laughter.

"Ready to die? That's a good one! Does it seem I am in the death throes? Or do you think I'm a criminal who will be guillotined at dawn? That's why you're forcing me to get out of bed at nine in the morning, like a street-sweeper? You took all this bother just to play this silly little joke? Well! Come on, my dear Father, are you sure you're quite well?"

"I could ask the same question of you, Madame—even though I cannot doubt I would be doing so in vain . . . I know what I'm saying." The priest spoke in a low voice, which seemed to make an impression on her. "I know it full well. Have you already forgotten what happened in church yesterday, between you and me?"

"I know, Monsieur, that you took my confession, the sacrament of penance, and that the secrets of confession are inviolable. That much I know—and nothing else."

There was silence.

"Therefore, I must inform you of what you do not know—or do not wish to know. So be it. You came and issued a frightful challenge to God. Not satisfied with profaning—hideously and out of malice alone—the sacrament you are so bold as to name, you have declared the intention of committing even greater sacrilege . . . Naturally, you were counting on the silence of an unfortunate priest bound by his holy office . . . I might respond that I have no obligation to keep the secret of a confession *that does not exist.* However, these forms are so sacred that even their outward likeness possesses the dignity of the act itself. And so I will say nothing.

"And yet, you are in danger, and it is my duty to warn you. There is still time . . . I entreat you by the Blood of Christ I have just now consumed. Do not force me to be your judge."

"Oh! But that's of no importance, Monsieur Blood-drinker. Judge me as much as you like. Having granted this indulgence, however, and since we're not exactly before the Revolutionary Tribunal, I in turn ask you to put an end to this tasteless joke. I am already quite tired of it, let me assure you."

"Then I shall leave," said the missionary. "This is all I have to say: challenge for challenge. I don't know what God will do with your soul, and I tremble to think of it. However, I sense that on Sunday *you will be unable* to perform the horrid act you announced to me from your pit of darkness. The glorious Christ is the bread of the poor, Madame, and to be eaten in the Light."

Conclusion.

On Easter Sunday, the church was full and Brunissende occupied the seigneurial pew reserved for her, more dazzling than ever.

The clergyman had insisted on celebrating this solemn mass. Having read the Gospel of Anointment and Resurrection, he shed his ornaments and appeared in the flesh.

He was extremely pale. In his surplice, he looked like the angel arrayed in white—the one the holy women saw at the Tomb.

Uncustomarily, he spoke on the words, *Edent pauperes et saturabuntur*: "The poor shall eat and be filled."

He spoke for about an hour, as if he were waiting until he ran out of breath—as if he hoped he would die from speaking. His voice rose higher and higher, until it became terrifying, luminous, and supernatural.

This man, who otherwise lacked eloquence, was sublime. He preached so fluently on poverty that the ragged audience appeared to be an assembly of the mighty; ultimately, the haughty Viscountess seemed like a wretch begging for bread.

When it came time for Easter communion, only the following occurred:

As the humble flock drew near, Brunissende—who had kneeled down first—jolted back suddenly, as if a wall of flames had shot up. The priest, approaching from the last step of the altar, bearing the ciborium toward the Holy Table, went back up abruptly . . .

The sanctuary had to be purified, and every year, on this selfsame day, a cleansing ceremony is scrupulously observed.

From then on, the Viscountess des Egards has seemed be alive, but in reality she is even more abject than the inhabitants of tombs . . .

That's how the political collapse of a preeminent puppet of the Moral Order was explained to me.

XXI.   It's Gonna Blow!

That night there were about ten of us, the newly elect of eternity, at the house of Henry de Groux, painter of murders.

We had arranged ourselves attentively so there would not be in our midst a single one of those who are destined for the academies—men whom derisory immortality can satisfy.

Our councils had firmly established that no one would ever admit the beginning or end of anything at all, nor descend to the abject state of thinking himself *fulfilled* by fortune of any kind.

We were the canons of the Infinite, the deacons of the Absolute, the consecrated executioners of all likely opinions and respected commonplaces. From time to time, I dare say, lightning struck us.

And thus, on that evening, after lavish and photogenic pronouncements on many a subject, it so happened that a unicorn-hunter—as opinionated as he was subtle, a man reputed both for his Hyrcanian doctrines and for his glabrous physiognomy—saw fit to declare as follows.

"Have you duly remarked, dear companions, the buffoonery of a higher nature in what are conventionally called Repressive Measures? Persistent and jubilatory statistics regularly inform us of the flux and ebb in infractions of our penal laws. We enjoy the synoptic catalogs to which are consigned—in Arabic numerals, of course—the murders and rapes that have helped us to endure the monotony of our days; these are the crimes the authorities have punished unremittingly from one age to the next.

"It would be idle, I submit, to contest the patriotic interest held by these documents, which customarily make dutiful philanthropists shudder from their spurs all the way up to their coxcombs.

"It would be no less interesting, you may agree without paling in indignation, to undertake to disclose the universal villainy of respectable people. Even highway robbers and the most infamous of thieves would rise in protest against such calumny heaped on those who stabilize the social order.

"However, I believe I shall make myself agreeable in sharing with you the poem of an altogether ordinary experiment that yielded significant results.

"Yesterday morning, as I walked down Rue Saint-Honoré, I discerned a venerable man who was descending the steps of Saint-Roch. He was such a gentle old soul he seemed to radiate warmth. Just looking at him felt like eating marrow of veal. From modest hands poured all the mildness of which he disposed; his delicate step lent him the air of a snowman made of sugar mincing on a rabbit's belly. The sky his friendly eye searched was—lest any doubt remain—his ally, his bosom friend. Surely, he had just performed exercises of devotion with incontestable piety and now, just as certainly, steered his course toward brotherly practices that the caresses of heaven alone will be adequate to reward—a little later on.

"Based on such examination, I concluded immediately that a consummately shady customer stood before me. I went up to him.

"'Monsieur,' I said in a hasty, muffled voice, 'Watch out! *It's gonna blow!*'

"You know I am not easily surprised. Well, my friends, the effect these words had unsettled me so profoundly that I spent a few hours in utter stupefaction.

"This character turned green, darted the wild, despairing glance of a Negro in the jaws of a crocodile, started shaking like a leaf, and leapt into a car, which vanished instantly.

"And that's what I have to tell you. I'm convinced that nineteen times out of twenty, a similar experiment—assuming it's properly conducted— would achieve the same result. It's up to you to try. Modern consciences stand so deeply indebted that anyone who is bold enough has the power to transform himself into a bolt of thunder and move like the Gorgon herself among the herds of the honorable."

꽃

"Gads!" shouted Rodolosse in his booming voice. "What timing, my good man. For the last few days I have had a confidential letter in my possession, which I'll to read you in a moment. I'm not the kind of cleric who preserves the secrets of confession; anyway, I'll stop at the signature. The author's admissions confirm and bear witness to the gladsome paradox we have just heard—and so much so I could not possibly deprive you of testimony so conclusive.

"The letter I hold," he went on (exhibiting a sheet of paper), "comes from a very well-known and perfectly honorable artist, you should know. Perfectly and absolutely ho-no-ra-ble.

Dear Sir,

A few days ago, you were so good as to remark in me a certain sadness that nothing can dispel, the cause of which eludes you. You insisted that I share it. Today, I am resolved to grant you satisfaction.

It is a terrible secret, and a fairly dangerous one, which I have guarded for fifteen years. It seems you have looked more deeply in me than others have. Perhaps you will not be too surprised. Maybe you will even feel a little compassion for a piteous individual the world deems happy, but who is continually rent asunder by appalling remorse.

No matter. I am sharing myself with you in the hope I shall be relieved of part of a burden that afflicts me more each passing day. One always winds up being forced to confess to someone, and I have chosen you so as not to succumb to the temptation of addressing the first policeman to happen by, since I lack the courage to seek out a priest.

Rest assured it will not take long.

In 187 . . . , I was twenty-five years old and crushed by poverty. At the time, there was nothing to suggest my future success or subsequent prosperity—for which the few poor devils who have inherited my straits envy me today. Then, I myself was consumed by the basest and most hateful invidiousness. I was keen on the beauty of my own soul and harbored no doubt about my genius. Could I suffer that vulgarians, consummate cretins, and incorrigible dunces possessed, with impunity, habitations, women, pigs, and potatoes—yet I, the greatest artist in the world, slept under the pavilion of the sterile heavens?

I had no domicile and no money—sometimes I didn't even have any pockets—and my adolescent gut remonstrated against the hard law of the most insatiable appetite.

Prompted by a trafficker in human flesh, I had taken up brokering policies on the lives of others; unable to get any leads, I was literally expiring from hunger out in the country, so I set out for Paris on nimble foot . . .

"At this point, messieurs," the reader said, "the details and circumstances of location are so precise that I am forced to pass over a reasonably large number of lines. At any rate, you have been sufficiently edified by my correspondent's spiritual bearing. So, without further ado, the denouement.

. . . It was August and the heat had been intolerable all day. Exhausted and unable to walk under the burning sun, I had slept, or tried to sleep, at the side of the road, under the shade of an immense millstone—the last in a long row reaching back to the barn of a farmstead where all hospitality had been brutally denied to me.

When I awoke, night had fallen. It was exquisite, without a trace of moonlight. It seemed I would easily manage to complete the four or five leagues still separating me from Paris. But I was so hungry I was about to cry.

I rummaged mechanically in the rags I was wearing for a stump of bread—a mouthful of anything at all—and lay hold of something I thought was an old crust. I immediately carried it to my mouth, bellowing in delight.

It was a box of matches.

I didn't swallow it—that accursed box, the villainous box whose presence I never have been able to explain; no doubt, demons had sent it.

At the same time, something laid hold of me—something better, it seemed, than stuffing my guts. I was glutted, drunk, and *refreshed* by the delectable wine of hatred and vengeance. I felt a light breeze blowing from the direction of the farmstead.

In half an hour, it was all ablaze. The unwelcoming house turned into a mass of cinders; later I learned that a crippled old woman was burnt to a crisp . . . The guilty party was never found . . .

When our friend Rodolosse reached this point, a sculptor whose silken beard I had been contemplating energetically turned the switch on the lamp shining upon us, and the sobs of *several* men filled the darkness.

XXII. The Silver Lining

"Please, have pity on a poor seer!"

The story was utterly banal. He had had the misfortune of receiving the gift of *clairvoyance* following a terrible disaster in which a great number of honest people lost their lives.

I believe it was a railway accident—unless it was a shipwreck, fire, or earthquake. No one ever did find out. He wouldn't speak about it willingly, and whatever subtle means one employed, he always managed to elude charitable parties' insulting curiosity.

I will always remember the imposingly ornamental presence of this suppliant under the basilical porch of Saint-Isidore-le-Laboureur, where he sought alms. For his ruin was absolute.

One could not but yield to the respectful compassion awakened by misfortune so rare and so nobly endured.

One sensed that once this individual had known (and better than many others, no doubt) the precious joys of blindness.

Surely a brilliant education had refined in him the inestimable ability to see nothing at all—the privilege of all mortals (almost without exception) and the deciding factor of their superiority over simple beasts.

Before the accident—one guesses with considerable emotion—he might have been one of those distinguished men deprived of sight who are called upon to decorate their homeland; indeed, from this epoch there remained in him the melancholy of a prince of darkness, now exiled in light.

All the same, offerings didn't exactly rain into the old hat he was always holding out to passersby. A beggar struck with such an extraordinary infirmity unsettled the munificence of the devout men and women who saw him and hastened to gain the sanctuary.

Instinctively, they distrusted this man in need, who saw the sun at high noon. It could only be explained by some exceptional crime—some sacrilege without name for which he now made atonement in this manner. From far away, parents pointed him out to their progeny as a living testament to the fearsome judgments of God.

For a time there was even fear of contagion, and the parish priest was set to evict him. Luckily, a group of honorable sages, whose authority no one could doubt, issued a declaration; with some bitterness but most peremptorily, they affirmed: "It isn't catching."

And so he lived meanly from rare alms and the slight fruit of the vain labors at which he excelled.

He had no match when it came to threading needles. He even threaded pearls with astonishing rapidity.

Indeed, I myself had been forced to enlist his services several times, in order to decipher the works of a reputable psychologist who had adopted the habit of writing with camel hairs split in four.

That is how we met, and how the regrettable intimacy formed which, one day, would cost me so dearly.

God keep me from being hard on a poor monster who now, moreover, lies long buried. All the same, one may judge what baneful influence was exercised on my young imagination by this individual, who taught me the magic secret—forgotten for so many centuries—of how to tell a lion apart from a pig, and the Himalayas from a pile of dust.

Such dangerous knowledge almost proved my undoing. It had taken but little for me to share my preceptor's destiny. I had gotten to the point where I hardly *groped* at all. That word there says it all.

My lucky star—thank Heaven!—saved me from the abyss. Little by little, I managed to free myself from his fateful ascendancy, break the charm once and for all, and still cut a reasonably good figure among the moles and patients of the Quinze-Vingts who play blindman's-buff with life.

But that happened over time—nothing but time, and still I was forced to hand over a considerable portion of my revenue to benefit from the famed dexterity of a Chicago oculist, who restored me to the light once and for all.

And yet, I wanted to know what had become of the terrible beggar. Behold exactly how he ended.

For a few more years he continued his clairvoyant begging at the cathedral door. His affliction, people said, grew with age. The older he got, the more clearly he saw. The alms decreased proportionately.

The vicars still gave him a few small coins to ease their conscience. Strangers, who suspected nothing, or creatures of the lowest depths—who, very probably, had the principle of clairvoyance in them, too—would assist him sometimes.

The blind man at the other door—a just and piteous man who earned well—extended his favor with a humble offering on days of celebration.

But all in all, it amounted to very little. Given the revulsion he inspired, which mounted every day, there was reason to speculate that it would not take him long to die of hunger.

One might have thought he had taken an oath. He paraded his infirmity cynically—as legless cripples, the goitrous, the ulcerated, amputees, and the rachitic display their misfortune at village festivals for the saints. He thrust it under your nose and, so to speak, forced you to inhale it.

The public's disgust and indignation had reached an apogee, and the bandit's fate was hanging by a single thread, when an event occurred that was just as prodigious as it was unexpected.

The clairvoyant received an inheritance from a grandnephew in America who had grown insolently rich by counterfeiting manure—and then was eaten by Araucanian cannibals.

The ex-beggar did not reclaim his relative's remains; instead, he took over the estate and began to live it up. One might have thought that the improbable and monstrous lucidity that had assured his fame would positively *rage*—just as tuberculosis leads to promiscuity. But the very opposite occurred.

A few months later, he was completely healed—and without an operation, either. He lost all clairvoyance and even went completely deaf.

Always pickled to high heaven, he had finally been delivered from the outer world by *the silver lining*.

XXIII.   A Well-Fed Man

Sir, I regret to inform you that Monsieur Venard Prosper, Room Bouley 13, passed away at 10 o'clock in the morning on 17 October 1893. I kindly request that you make known to me your intentions relating to the burial of the body, which should be removed within twenty-four hours, and that you also provide the necessary documents (birth or marriage certificate) to draw up the death certificate in keeping with the law.

Last month, this notice issued by Hôpital Necker informed me of the inglorious demise of one of the most well-fed men ever observed beneath the mountains of the moon, comparable only to the great gluttons of the Touraine in the epics of Rabelais.

I had the distinction of being his friend, and I am proud to have shared in some of his feasts. However, I don't know how it so happened that I was the only one left of a great host when the inexplicable marasmus occurred that consumed him at the age of thirty-five. The poor man had no one but me to visit him in his last days—or to attend to his funeral.

I did the best I could. I am happy to have saved his body from the odious profanations of the operating theater and the terrifying final insult of the crematory, where the ever-maternal state welfare service sees to it that indigents who have died in its lairs are burned without their permission.

That is, the poor don't even own their own carcass; lying in the hospital after a desperate soul has fled, the piteous and precious body promised to eternal resurrection—O suffering Christ!—is carried off without a cross or a prayer, far from your churches and your altars, far from the consolations of those beautiful stained glass windows depicting your holy allies, to serve, like the carrion of unclean beasts, the experiments of pork butchers and manufacturers of dust . . .

Pardon me. I've forgotten that this story is in fact overflowing with consolation—I should hope that even the most disappointed optimists will not read it without finding it to contain at least some tenderness.

My friend Venard practiced, with a certain genius, the most forgotten of arts. No mere *illustrator*, he revived Illumination itself—and was one of the greatest contemporary artists.

He told me he had practiced a reasonably serious study of draftsmanship in his youth; much later, his singular vocation was revealed to him when, returning from a celebrated expedition on which he almost died only to find that his inheritance had vanished, poverty compelled him to seek a way of earning a living.

At all stages of life, this man of action had been bound to the abilities he possessed; mechanically, he sought to confound them by turning his hand to heteroclitic ornaments with which, in his hours of ponderous leisure, he overloaded the surprisingly terse letters he wrote to friends and mistresses.

There were messages from him announcing a rendezvous that were only three words long, in which amorous elucubrations were replaced by a hedge of arabesques, impossible clusters of leaves, inextricable mazes, and monstrous faces colored most unusually, in which the few syllables giving voice to his fancy met the eye in Carolingian uncials or Anglo-Saxon characters—the two most energetic scripts after the rectilinear capitals of consulary calendars.

A gothic contempt for all modern contrivances had given him the need, the impassioned taste, for these venerable forms; his thought entered them as his limbs might have slipped into a suit of armor.

Little by little, decorative letters had inspired ambition for *historiated initials*, then for miniatures detached from the text, with all that this entailed in keeping with the way the one, primordial art generated the others: it had started with Merovingian monks making modest transcriptions, and it culminated, after half a dozen centuries, in Van Eyck, Cimabue, and Orcagna—all of whom extended work with vivid colors onto canvas, which the Renaissance then used to abuse the aesthetic traditions of the more spiritual Middle Ages.

His aptitude became positively prodigious as soon as he decided to take full advantage of his gift, and he emerged as a marvelous artist of unforeseen originality.

He studied with care and consulted without cease the delectable monuments preserved at the Bibliothèque Nationale and the Archives: the evangelaries of Charlemagne, Charles the Bald, and Lothar, the psalter of Saint Louis, the sacramentarium of Drogon de Metz, the celebrated books of hours of René of Anjou and Anne of Brittany, as well as the sublime miniatures by Jehan Fouquet, the official painter of Louis XI.

He almost resorted to baseness to be granted permission to copy a few biblical scenes and landscapes from the splendid Book of Hours formerly owned by the brother of Charles V, now in the possession of the Duke of Aumale.

Finally, one day, he made the costly pilgrimage to Venice, simply so he might inspect the miraculous Grimani Breviary, to which Memling is thought to have contributed, and from which Dürer drew inspiration.

All the same, he never reproduced—save by juxtaposing fragments—the work of his medieval predecessors. His compositions were always strange and unexpected, whether Flemish, Irish, Byzantine, or even Slavic—entirely his own and in no one else's style. It was his, "the Venard style," as Barbey d'Aurevilly aptly put it in the glowing review that established the illuminator's reputation.

Because he scorned the chloroses of aquarelle, his unique method involved painting with unmixed gouache and heightening the violence of the colors in relief through the application of a varnish he had invented, and whose composition he permitted no one to analyze.

Consequently, his illuminations had the brilliance and luminous consistency of enamel. They offered a feast to the eyes, as well as a powerful ferment of reverie to imaginations still capable of lifting up the chimera's tail and returning to bygone ages.

I must still explain how this extraordinary personage was so well fed—and why his lamentable end offered the opportunity for so many others to find consolation.

As is well known, I never miss a chance to let my contemporaries' merits shine; it is a matter of necessity for me to apply the balm of my adjectives to bleeding hearts.

In this blessed instance, there is almost nothing for me to do. Indeed, I wonder whether moral grandeur has ever been as radiant as on the occasion of the illuminator's passing.

Prosper Venard had not yet been buried when, already, some twenty pages composed by right-minded authors lamented the little-known reason for his demise.

The illuminator had thought only of eating. For ten years, no one had seen him do anything, so to speak, except look for food. It seemed the public coffers would have had to be emptied to satisfy his cravings, and all the flocks of Mesopotamia would have scarcely sufficed to meet the voracity of the departed.

Now—by the grace of God!—it was finished. The cyclone of ravenous appetite had dissipated. It was finally admitted that other mortals should exercise their lower mandibles, and, delivered from peril so great, French society could calmly return to the table.

The revelations poured in. "I fed him for two years," said the one. "He was always coming to eat at my house," cried the other. "I never saw him once that he didn't complain he was dying of hunger," a third vociferated.

To universal stupefaction, it was discovered that absolutely everyone, without exception, had stuffed the gullet of said Venard. Over five hundred parties, it seemed, had busied themselves with nothing but filling him up from morning to night; if he had succumbed to torpor—as the head of medical services at the hospital attested so strangely—it's because there was simply nothing to be done, it was much wiser to give up, and so on.

"Let's cut to the chase," one of our most adipose critics averred. "It's disheartening. It's profoundly inequitable. At least we have a right to the lard of pigs fed at such a great expense. This gentleman couldn't muster gratitude of even the coarsest variety."

Well, it's true. I won't deny that my friend, the *lean* Venard, ate well enough when he had the chance—and I believe this occurred just a little less frequently than Neptune and Jupiter stand in alignment. However, he didn't know how to *lick* as well as he might have.

It never was possible to impress on him that an impoverished artist has the duty to lick at the soles of any literary runt who ever regaled him with peels and rinds—and that the greater an artist he is, the more it behooves him to do so.

Even less did he appreciate that a loan of a hundred sous committed him, for all eternity, to the jackassery of perpetual deference. He lacked respect for the mighty men who disgusted him; hence his reputation for ingratitude.

I sought to defend him. I even made bold to declare it possible, all things considered, that a few meals lacking in sumptuousness might be repaid, a million times over, by incomparably magnificent works of illumination—works no one mentioned even in a whisper, which this exile from the Middle Ages had simply given to his *benefactors*.

In turn, I was told to keep quiet: this big eater's polychromatic extravagances were unsellable and wouldn't yield any interest until the latter half of the twentieth century—the epoch a few prophets had designated for the resurrection of Barbarossa, or maybe Charlemagne.

As we await such a day, his legend flourishes. Perhaps the dukes and margraves that will emerge from the guts of Anarchy and rule over Europe in a hundred years will grant whole regions in exchange for a few miniatures by this Venard—a greedy man notorious for having depleted his unfortunate peers, who only sought to feed him well.

XXIV.   The Lucky Bean

A handsome young man and a beautiful young girl are en-
thusiastically married. After the ceremony—*alone at
last!*—they sit facing one another on comfortable chairs.
They look at each other for a long time without saying a
word and die of horror.

Handbook of Contemporary Life

Monsieur Tertullian had just turned fifty; his hair was still a handsome
black, his affairs were proceeding admirably, and the esteem he enjoyed
grew from day to day, when he had the misfortune of losing his wife.

The blow was terrible. One would have to be perverse to imagine a
more obliging companion.

Twenty years younger than her husband, she had had the most appetizing face in the world and a personality so delicious she never once missed
an opportunity to delight.

The magnanimous Tertullian had married her without a dime—as do
most merchants inconvenienced by bachelorhood, who don't have time to
waste on seducing intractable virgins.

He had married her "between two cheeses," he used to say cheerfully.
For he traded cheese in bulk, and the weighty act had been solemnized in
the interval between a memorable delivery of Chester and an exceptional
load of Parmesan.

This union, I regret to say, had not borne fruit, and it cast a shadow on the elegant tableau.

Who was to blame? The grave question hung heavy among the fruit sellers and grocers of Gros-Caillou. A bristly butcher, whom the handsome Tertullian once had scorned, baldly accused him of impotence—in defiance of objections voiced by a grainy woman who manufactured mattresses and claimed to be fully licensed.

The pharmacist, however, averred that one should wait before formulating an opinion, and the kindly assembly of concierges, who viewed the item of contention with impartiality, applauded the thinker's circumspection.

They, in turn, observed with great authority that Paris had not been built in a day, all's well that ends well, to travel far one must fit one's saddle, etc., etc.; consequently, there was cause to anticipate a favorable event that, at one point or another, would add the final touch to the dazzling prosperity of the cheese merchant.

One might have thought the matter concerned a dauphin of France.

Emotions ran high when people learned that sudden death had cut down such worthy hopes.

Unless Tertullian remarried promptly—a hypothesis that his grief made it impossible to entertain for even a single minute—the future of his establishment was hashed, and this self-made man, who was already so rich even though he had started with nothing, would ultimately see his clientele defect to a foreign successor!

Such a bleak prospect must have singularly worsened the woes of the mournful husband.

Indeed, it seemed the latter stood ready to tumble headlong into a pit of despair.

I don't know the extent to which the dream of a cheesy heir acted upon him, but I was earwitness to his roars of grief and to extrajudiciary summons he issued to himself: that he should follow his Clementine to the grave in short order (without, for all that, fixing a deadline).

I had the leisure to make a thorough study of this likeable man, with whom I entertained the closest commercial relations for ten years. There were many occasions to observe a character trait that was admirable, if little known.

He had an appalling fear of being cuckolded. For two or three hundred years, this fate had befallen all his ancestors, and to a great extent, the tenderness he showed his wife stemmed from his unshakable confidence in her emphatic assurances that the integrity she presented stood beyond doubt.

His *gratitude* even had something profoundly comical and touching about it. In retrospect, it seems to have been almost tragic. Sometimes, in stupefaction, I would ask myself whether Clementine's scandalous sterility could be explained otherwise than by certain, rather odd suspicions that Tertullian harbored about his *own identity*—and by his sublime fear that he might be cuckolding himself if he fertilized her.

But that was all too lofty—too far up over the clouds, the curds, and the whey. Instead, the inevitably banal event that had to happen, happened.

When Clementine restored her soul to the Lord, the wretched widower first, and with due gustiness, exhaled the moans and sobs that nature recommends.

After he had made this initial offering (if I may employ an expression he preferred), he wanted to set the relics of his beloved in order—before the burial ceremony, which promised a crowd that made him bristle well in advance.

There, his cruel fate awaited him. The opprobrious standard of the Tertullian clan appeared before his eyes.

In an obscure drawer of an intimate piece of furniture that this most sensitive of husbands had never thought to suspect, he discovered correspondence as voluminous as it was varied, which didn't let him catch his breath for even a second.

All his friends and acquaintances were there. With the sole exception of myself, his wife had cherished every one of them.

At the same time, even his employees—he found missives from employees on pink paper—had found her favor.

He acquired certainty that his late wife had deceived him day and night, under all meteorological conditions, and more or less everywhere: in his bed, in his cellar, in his attic, in his store—even under the watchful eye of the Gruyere and amidst the exhalations of the Roquefort and Camembert.

It would be idle to add that these impure exchanges hardly soothed him. They mocked him endlessly, from the first line to the last.

An agent of the telegraph exchange who was famous for his subtle wit made fun of him for how he conducted his business—and in a manner as offensive as possible; he even took the liberty of making allusions and offering *advice* unfit for print.

Yet there was something else: something unheard of, exorbitant, and phenomenal—enough to bring the stars of Capricorn out of alignment.

The mortifying dossier had an appendix: an interminable array of little sticks, which surprised him and at first seemed inexplicable. He summoned the sagacity of a cunning Apache crouching over the enemy's trail. A blinding light inundated him as he realized that the number of these objects precisely matched the number of admirers his faithless wife had rallied—and that each one had bountiful *scores* made with a penknife, like the marks bakers use to record sales.

Obviously, Clementine had been a lady of the higher order, and she held tightly to this position.

Crushed by humiliation, the husband expressed the wholly natural desire that he be left alone with the deceased, and for two or three hours, he locked himself away—like a man who means to abandon himself to grief without reserve.

A few weeks later, Tertullian offered a sumptuous dinner on the Eve of Epiphany.

Twenty male guests, who had been selected carefully, crowded around the table. The host had deployed magnificence beyond compare. The fare was exquisite, abundant, and unusual. It seemed like the farewell feast of an opulent prince who was preparing to abdicate.

For all that, several in attendance experienced a moment of unease on account of the funereal quality of the décor; no doubt, the cheese merchant's imagination had grown gloomy, and he had borrowed the setting from some melodrama he once had seen.

The walls and even the ceiling were covered in black. The tablecloth was black. There were black candelabras, and black candles burned. Everything was black.

The employee of the telegraph exchange was completely unnerved, and he wanted to leave. A cheery pig farmer held him back. One should "be up for anything," he said—he thought it was "rich."

After a moment of indecision, the others resolved to turn up their noses at death. Soon, bottles were passing freely, and the meal became quite gay. When the champagne was served, punning had the upper hand and the trash talk started. Then, a gigantic cake was brought in.

"Messieurs," said Tertullian as he rose, "Let us empty our glasses, if you please, to the memory of our beloved dead. Each one of you had the chance to know, and appreciate, her loving heart. Surely you haven't forgotten her loving, tender heart? And so I ask that you fill yourselves, in a *most special* way, with her memory before this king cake—which she would have so loved to share with you—is divided."

Having never been the lover of the cheesemonger's wife—if only because I never met her—I had not been invited to the dinner. Thus, I cannot know to whom the charmed bean fell.

However, I do know that the diabolical Tertullian had some trouble with the law for having placed, in the enormous flanks of this almond-paste confection, the heart of his wife—the rotten little *heart* of his delicious Clementine.

XXV. Digestive Aids

All bellies were full. It was resolved to do away with the poor.

At ten o'clock of an evening, some thirty sublime plantigrades had agreed that the brotherly "seesawing" had dragged on for too many centuries: it was meet to heap ample reprobation on the ragged class that takes malicious pleasure in tearing at the heartstrings of the well-dressed.

Various motions were expectorated.

The Psychologist cooed that nothing is as beautiful as compassion— the truthful and judicious compassion stirred by the groaning of the rich— and that it is a crime against society to encourage beggarly sloth.

He added that an enlightened government would be concerned above all with protecting—against the latter—the genteel understanding and "spiritual subtlety" that preserve for us the traditions of aristocratic elegance and feeling.

Francisque Lepion, a philosopher fat and full of energy, belched out the conclusion, summarily declaring that any French citizen unable to prove a yearly income of thirty thousand francs should be sent to penal colonies most insalubrious.

A man liberated from mischance in Constantinople, who had achieved celebrity by performing the song of nightingales at the Sixtine Chapel of universal suffrage, applauded this equitable vow with tibicen chirping.

Several mucilaginous and convoluted poets enumerated the dire punishments that vigorous measures of repression should enact on the impenitent and recidivous poor.

Successive cries of enthusiasm hailed firing squads, machine-gunnings, drownings, *autos-da-fé*, banishments en masse, and deportations.

It so happened that a booklover had brought with him the extremely rare first edition of the famed *Cartulary of Excruciations*, composed in fourteen languages and printed toward the beginning of the ninth century at King-Tcheou-Fou, on the banks of the Xiang River, by the Plantin of the Celestial Empire. He read a few pages, and his listeners shed tears of emotion.

There would be no end were I to report the transcendental apophthegms offered on this occasion by the women who attended in their finery—whose reason, as every one knows, surpasses that of men so greatly.

At any rate, isn't it enough to inform the gentle reader that it all happened at the residence of the refulgent Vidamesse du Fondement, whose most fortunate spouse had been crowned in glory when he negotiated the bilateral agreement—long considered an unattainable dream by the cabinets of Europe—henceforth uniting (at last!) the Principality of Sodom and the French Republic?

My historian's conscience will not allow me to omit mention of an individual—a bizarre and fairly inscrutable party—whose precarious attire offered a surprise in such a milieu.

His familiars knew him as Apemantus, and he was the Cynic. This precious quality conferred on him a measure of welcome in certain groups of utmost sophistication pretending to supreme Athenianism.

"What do you live on?" he once had been asked maliciously—in the presence of fifty others—by the most vinegary of poetesses.

"On alms, madam," he replied simply—with the coolness of a dead fish.

The response (which was, in fact, imprecise) describes his character quite well.

No one bothered him much, for he was known to have a vicious bite; sometimes he brandished a kind of barbarous eloquence that compelled the notice of even the most inattentive and retractile or the most constipated and ethereal.

In a word, he said whatever he liked—a rare privilege that no one contested.

And so, that night, the mistress of the house asked him to manifest his sentiments.

"Too bad, then. It'll be quite the tale," said Apemantus. "As disagreeable a tale as ever was, it goes without saying. But first, you must endure—without understanding in the least, I should think—a few reflections, or preliminary conjectures, that I need in order to rouse the narrator in me.

"Unfortunately, there's no denying that poverty contaminates the world's beaming countenance, and it's entirely deplorable that ladies redolent of perfume should so often be exposed to run-ins with small children dying of hunger.

"I know one may employ the expedient of not seeing them. Yet all the same, one senses they exist. Their inharmonious pleas afflict the ear, and there's even the risk of catching some tiny pest. You are quite familiar, dear ladies, with the vile, pedicular vermin that 'does not let itself be petted as willingly as an elephant,' as the great poet Maldoror said: this creature on its own will abandon the needy with good conscience to creep into muffs and furs of inestimable value.

"The whole matter plunges me into bitterest affliction—and so I applaud, to the point of delirium, the lofty idea of a general holocaust of the indigent.

"All the same—and until the good news of massacres arrives—I ask leave to inquire of those among you who have never scratched yourselves: have you had occasion to observe, without a telescope, the unequal distribution of philosophical certainty concerning a few so-called axioms?

"To put things a little differently: where can one find a man—one who has not yet been certified and cataloged as a native idiot or senile—

who will dare say he has no shadow of a doubt about his own *identity*? For that is the point.

"Quite naïvely, I affirm that, having betimes reflected on what the Gospels tell—that an astonishing multitude of swine was needed to house the impure demons that had issued from a single man—I occasionally look around and feel terror . . ."

"Pardon, monsieur," interjected a paleographer, "but it seems you're going a bit far."

"Well, then. I'm headed in the right direction!" the unshakable man replied, leaning forward. "That's just it. I want to go far."

"Let's see," he resumed good-naturedly. "I shall deign to make myself entirely clear. What, in our most esteemed literature—and by that I mean the serialized novel or the theater—what, I say, is paramount, irresistible, indestructible, primordial, and fundamental?

"What, if I dare express myself in this way, is the string on which everything hangs, the great mystery, the 'Open, Sesame!' that unlocks the caverns of pathos, divinely and infallibly making the masses shudder and thrill?

"My God! What I'm about to tell you is really quite simple. The grand secret, simply put, is *uncertainty about personal identity*.

"There's always somebody who is not—or might not be—the party one supposes. It's always necessary to have a son no one suspected to exist, a mother no one knows about, or an uncle, more or less noble, who has to be gotten out of some mess.

"Finally, everyone recognizes each other: behold the wellspring of tears. It hasn't changed since Sophocles.

"Don't you think—as I do—that the immortal power of such a banal idea connects with some symbol, a *premonition* lying very deep, toward which, for three thousand years, the tellers of tales have groped in the dark, like the blinded Oedipus desperately seeking the hand of his Antigone? . . .

"We were talking about the poor, weren't we? Well here we are. The mechanism of emotion is unthinkable without the Poor Man—without his intervention and perpetual presence; and so, I appeal that he be maintained and continue to exist in the theater and novels.

"The rich man, on the other hand, can't pretend to have any kind of 'catch.' It's impossible to hide him, because he's at home everywhere. His presence is blinding, and his identity oozes from every pore—at least in literature. The universe gawks at him, and God Himself is at such pains to come up with a part for the rich man in his *Mysteries* that He has simply left him the worn-out and trivial practice of charity.

"And so, if it is necessary—indeed, imperative—that slaughter occur, I make bold to propose that it happen after a prefatory process of evaluation: the conclusive and irrefragable verification of individuals."

"The anthropometry of souls, that is," specified the Psychologist (who was quite bored).

"That lousy phrase—or any other one. Fine. At any rate, you'd need the crucible of God. May the Devil drag me off if anyone—here or anywhere else—can write himself a passport worth anything at all.

"No one knows his own *name*, and no one even knows his own true face, because no one knows the mysterious being (and maybe it's one the worms are devouring) from which his *essence* derives."

"You're making fun of us, Apemantus," Madame du Fondement interjected. "You promised us a tale."

"So you insist. Fine.

"A wealthy man had two sons. The younger of them said to his father: 'Father, give me the portion of goods that falleth to me.' And the father divided unto them his living. And not many days after the younger son gathered all together, he took his journey into a far country, and there wasted his substance with riotous living . . .'"

"Ah! But that"—heatedly exclaimed the little Baroness de Carcan d'Amour (who devised the fashion of the plunging neckline beneath the navel), "That's the parable of the Prodigal Son this gentleman is handing us. Next, he'll say that his hero wound up tending swine and was dying of hunger; then, one day, he grew weary and returned to the house of his father—who was quite moved when he saw him from afar."

"Alas, no, Madame!" responded Apemantus in a very grave voice, "*It was the pigs that came . . .*"

That's where the conversation stood when Someone who didn't smell very good entered the room.

XXVI. The Reading Room

Literature is fundamental.

"Come on, damn it! Don't you know people are waiting?"

Orthodoxie Panard, who had been fiercely clutching the knob, took flight when she heard the dreaded voice of her paternal uncle.

This reading room was so comically arranged that just one person could use it at a given moment, and the house had ten residents.

They were Father Panard and Mother Panard, the four Panard heirs—Athanasius, Heliodorus, Demetrius, and Orthodoxie—then Uncle Justinian, Aunt Plectrude, and Aunt Roxelane. Finally, there was Palmyra, the old serving woman. That made ten in all. It was absurd.

Nota bene that all these people—including Palmyra, even—had (or could have had) intellectual needs of the most imperious nature.

At any hour of the day, there was sure to be someone. Sometimes, there was even a crowd at the door.

It was enough to make you sick of the family in general.

It proved impossible to make Panard, that skinflint, hear reason. A retired teacher of Greek—a member of the Institute, if you please—he never even washed his hands, for reasons of economy. Whenever anyone approached him about constructing a second location, he would declaim the curses of Hecuba—the same ones found in Euripides.

For all that, he didn't lack money; ever since he, this translator of Philostrates, had come into a significant inheritance, he had been a landholder of note.

Still, the modern literature that the Panards born of his rib fed on held no interest for him. He claimed everyone was content with the facilities as they existed and pretended not to hear the optative insinuations of his lineal descendants.

The most intolerable of contenders was Uncle Justinian. A retired colonel in the gendarmerie, he was never done.

Once this brute had managed to gain entry, supplications and tears were bootless. One simply had to wait a whole hour for him to finish rummaging about in the papers.

If only this scrap of leather—the fetid and senile man who never finished, this broken-down pimp of the guillotine—had possessed elevated motives for prolonging his vacation in this manner, for loitering indefinitely in the precious cabinet three or four times a day!

But no. This veteran of misfortune, whom the heavens refused to confound, never read anything but the particulars of wanted men and orders of arrest.

"What can you be doing in there? Merciful God!" cried Aunt Plectrude as she raised her withered arms toward the stars. (He often rose in the dead of night.)

"I'm attending to correspondence," he responded with the delicacy of a policeman one never catches off guard.

Orthodoxie suffered more than anyone else. She was a young lady of uncommon grace and cultivated literary contacts, and took cycling lessons.

Her brother Athanasius—who was already getting a start in Symbolism—had introduced her to the leader of the Romano-Spada school. His Greek roots earned him an exceptional welcome on the part of Panard *père*, and the sensible man quickly took advantage of such an accommodating attitude to sneak in his inseparable friend, the great Papadiamantopoulos.

Indeed, one day the professor let his well-founded guard down to such an extent that a man beyond all compare gained entry: the exalted Peritoneus, who deigned to come as he was, without any bother at all, crowned in the glory of his work.

Finally, because the symposium had assumed such vast dimensions, several *klephts* received asylum—for the love of Pindus.

Truly, the swelling tide of dinner guests made it even harder to use the reading facilities. Moreover, Justinian occupied the chamber as vexingly as ever, only emerging to make unforgivably ill-chosen remarks at the table.

This detail cast a shadow on the whole painting. It bears repeating: Orthodoxie experienced torment in the innermost fibers of her being.

The lovely girl asked only to open up and grow! The slightest breeze, and she would have spread wide in full flower! How easy would it have been, without her father's abject miserliness, to thrust in full vigor into the rapturous world where such worthy masters would be her sponsors!

Alas, such boldness would amount to schism with the patriarch and his prejudices—one already disquieted by the influx of apostles and who even spoke of dismissing Attica and the Peloponnese.

She anxiously saw the day approaching when she would have no choice but to pursue an education on her own, as before . . .

Ah! If only Panard had agreed to let her acquaint herself with the brilliant efforts of psychologists and mages! But the very idea was impossible. All the new works that authors and editors sent, with dedicatory inscriptions, to the inflexible member of the Institute immediately landed in that tiny cabinet, where one didn't even have a quarter of an hour to oneself.

There was no getting around it, either: it was the only way. It was impossible to make any progress elsewhere. There was no hope of taking instructive manuals to another location. The old man, who rooted about everywhere, would have exploded in rage if anyone had gotten the idea of hijacking a single volume from this private library, the whole catalog of which he had implacably memorized. The holdings simply had to be used on site.

Well, Justinian abused them scandalously. Whenever he consulted studies of customs and anthologies of verse, he left the pages in such a state that one could only utter a groan and give up on using them oneself. Not even the dedications were safe.

It drove poor, sentimental Orthodoxie out of her mind that she couldn't take up where she had left off; suddenly, she would find herself deprived of a chapter that would have enlightened her, no doubt. Despite her lack of experience, she was forced to come up with improbable episodes on her own and entertain conjectures about impossible climaxes.

꩜

Necessity, the saying goes, is the mother of invention. This veracious account will offer the proof.

One day, it happened that a sturdy deliveryman brought the complete works of the celebrated Russian novelist Borborygmus, who finally had been translated.

For quite some time, the young girl had dreamt of reading the emollient and philharmonic pages of the lax Muscovite. But it was easy to foresee that the precious mass would not escape the fate shared by the other lyrical and documentary papers that flowed without cease into the reading chamber.

To avert catastrophe, not a moment could be lost. And so, Orthodoxie went directly to Aunt Roxelane, who was also hooked on literature—and, after the young girl, surely the most finely tuned member of the family.

She was no less covetous than Panard, moreover; the latter thoroughly respected her for the handsome capital she possessed and employed so skillfully. She alone escaped the maniac's inquisition, and her dominion was respected.

In the flash of an eye, the conspiracy was hatched. The two women decreed that the great man would escape desecration at the hands of the colonel; Palmyra, whom they bought with illusory assurances, lugged the parcel into Roxelane's room.

Thereupon they spent a few happy days together—aunt and niece, reading and crying in concert . . .

Unfortunately, the sonorous Orthodoxie could not restrain her enthusiasm. Unbeknownst to her, Slavic ideas and metaphors came out; one fine morning, Panard's suspicions were roused.

The careless girl emitted a foreign sound when she thought she was talking sense. He surged from the table like a man struck out of the blue and dashed into the reading room at the very moment the relentless Justinian emerged.

For quite some time, he was heard energetically rummaging in the archives. The tempest loomed so near that no one dared move.

Finally, he reappeared, pale and red at once—rather like embers not yet extinguished upon which the North Wind blows.

"Where is my Borborygmus?" he yelled.

Alive to the commotion, Aunt Plectrude sought to steer the cyclone toward Justinian. The latter swore—by the cross and the boots on his feet—that he was held in unjust suspicion, and the truthfulness of this officer of the law could not be doubted.

Orthodoxie, in turn, was filled with terror and accused her brothers Athanasius, Heliodorus, and Demetrius. They didn't have the slightest idea what was going on, and the clear-eyed patriarch discerned their innocence without difficulty.

It was a serious case, and the punishment matched the crime. Restitution of the precious books had to occur; without delay, they followed the same path as their predecessors. The uncle, three times odious, had almost exclusive use of them. The writings had such an effect on him that he barely emerged from his lair except to eat.

But Orthodoxie, whose grief was heartbreaking, managed to find consolation all the same. Ultimately, she understood that such judgment awaits all mortal works, that that's how reading generally proceeds in families governed by reason, and that tangible pleasures count for far more than the deceptive elucubrations of a few dreamers . . .

But what am I saying? Hadn't she realized, above all, the profound truth of the axiom that one of our lady poets had formulated? Henceforth, it was be her guiding light:

Before opening your mouth, think long—and hard.

XXVII.   Nobody's Perfect

Asclepius Nuptial, making quite sure that the old man had received an adequate number of stabs and had definitively exhaled what convention calls "the last gasp," immediately turned his thoughts to obtaining a little diversion.

This circumspect individual reckoned that a rope always under pressure cannot hold, that a breath of fresh air often proves salutary, and that all labors merit compensation.

It was his good fortune to have landed on a real score. Happy to be alive and with his conscience delicately perfumed, he strolled here and there, beneath the chestnut and plane trees, inhaling with delight the fragrant breath of evening.

It was springtime—not the dubious and rheumatic spring of the equinox, but the heady renewal of the first days in June, when the Twins who embrace each other fade before the Crawfish.

Asclepius, bathing in suave sensations and his eyes moist with tears, felt like an apostle.

He wished happiness upon the human race, fraternity to savage beasts, guidance for the oppressed, and consolation to all who suffer.

Full of clemency, his heart inclined toward the needy. Into outstretched hands he poured the abundant copper coins that weighed heavy in his pockets.

He even entered a church and shared in the common prayer the loyal flock recited.

He voiced his adoration of God, telling Him he loved his neighbor as he did himself. He offered thanks for the goods he had received, humbly acknowledging he had been made from nothing.

He asked Him to dispel the darkness concealing the ugliness and malice of sin, performed a scrupulous examination of his conscience, and discovered clinging faults and noisome trifles: instances of vanity, impatience, distraction, oversight, rash and uncharitable judgment, and so on—but certainly sloth and neglect when performing the *duties of his estate*.

In conclusion, he resolved firmly to be less weak henceforth, implored the heavens to assist those dying or wandering abroad, and asked (as is fitting) for protection during the darkness of night. Then, penetrated by these sentiments, he scampered off to the nearest whorehouse.

For he preferred simple pleasures. He was not one to give himself over, in undue fashion, to frivolous dissipation.

If anything, he tended toward discipline—so much so that he barely avoided a laughably earnest appearance.

If he killed for a living, well, every trade has its value. Like so many others, he might have taken pride in the dangers attending this thorny profession. However, he thought silence better. Like the convolvulus, the flowers of his soul bloomed only in the shade.

He killed at home: politely, discreetly, and as tidily as possible. Indeed, one may affirm he did a good job.

He didn't make promises he couldn't keep. In fact, he didn't make promises at all. For all that, his customers had never complained.

He paid no mind to what venomous tongues hissed. *Do right and fear no man*, such was his motto. The voice of his own conscience was enough for him.

He was really a homebody. Only rarely was he spotted in cafes, and even the spiteful had to give him his due: when not in the brothel, he saw almost no one.

Here, in this hospitable environment, he focused his affection on a scantily clad young lady who assured the prosperity of commerce; the virtuosity she displayed beyond her years inspired general enthusiasm.

Hardly had she emerged from childhood but numerous salons admired her skills.

Lucky Asclepius had managed to make himself dear to her; time seemed to "suspend its flight" when the two beings tilted, the one toward the other, over the mystical lake.

As soon as her little Cucu appeared, the ravishing Lulu dropped whatever she was doing; indeed, the former was often compelled to remind her to return to a more professional bearing when elderly gentlemen grew impatient.

In exchange, she gave him precious tips . . .

All in all, they made some solid investments together. Lulu hardly required anything; air and light were more or less enough for her daily *toilette*, which was always very simple and in impeccable taste.

Already they could anticipate their reward: a happy future in the countryside, a cottage nestled beneath lilacs and roses they would one day buy, and the peaceable old age with which Providence repays those who have fought bravely.

Yes, no doubt, but, alas! Who shall tell of the vanity of mortal designs?

What follows is painful beyond measure.

That night, Asclepius did not show up. The establishment suffered for it more than words can say.

Poor Lulu was at first feverish, then restless, and finally distraught. She became disobliging.

A Belgian attorney (who had brought along his clients' funds) landed a pair of smacks; the loud report shocked parties nearby.

The scandal was huge, and imminent disgrace loomed large. All the same, she "wouldn't listen to anyone or anything." Her anguish escalated into delirium. She disregarded the law to such an extent that she flung open a window that had remained closed since 14 July the previous year. She bellowed a ghastly cry into the silence of night, calling for her Cucu.

A few Protestant pastors took flight for havens abroad after duly expressing their indignation; the following day, serious journals were predicting the end of the world.

Need I say it? Asclepius was painting the town red; he had met with a serpent.

As he was sensibly returning to the loving fold, an acquaintance from his childhood had accosted him, a man he hadn't seen for ten years, and who managed to bring him off the straight and narrow for the first time in his life.

I don't know what sophistry this baneful friend deployed to divert him from the path to heaven, but they got so drunk that, as dawn was breaking, the beloved of the languishing Lulu fell out of his orbit. He took a car to go look for the *Spiritual Combat* he remembered having forgotten at the corpse's lodgings the previous evening—something he deemed absolutely indispensable to his inner progress.

His trusty companion of the night led him, practically by the hand, all the way to the dead man's room, where the police commissioner was obligingly waiting for him.

And so did a single lapse wreck two careers.

Nobody's perfect.

XXVIII.   Let's Be Reasonable!

"Why won't you eat, father?" Suzanne asked, her eyes filled with tears. "For two days you haven't touched a thing and won't see anyone. You're not sick: you'd have called the doctor. What weighs so greatly on your heart that you won't share it? I'm not a little girl anymore, you know; let me comfort you!"

This discourse addressed a party no less distinguished than the celebrated Ambroise Chaumontel, a man whose affairs concerned half the globe—the peerless lawyer whose eloquence could tie up the fibers of Chaos itself and petrify Darkness.

The esquire was about sixty years old, and he didn't mince words. He issued his proclamations directly—no matter to whom, no matter the occasion—for he gently aspired to the dignity of the patriarchs.

Some poison-tongued rivals accused him of tinting his hair *white* in order to appear more venerable when pleading on behalf of orphans. He, however, kept his soul at an elevation infinitely higher than their envy, and so the darts landed feebly at his feet.

Over a quarter century spent at the bar, he had gained a fearsome reputation, vast riches, and a splendorous name that several loudmouthed generations had echoed; between him and the lowly multitude there lay a vast, unpassable expanse.

Finally, he enjoyed a kind of consideration altogether English, which nothing seemed able to diminish. No doubt for good reason, he counted as a party less than stimulating, but infinitely praiseworthy for professional integrity.

On that day, strange worries indeed must have preoccupied him, for he didn't answer his daughter. Instead, he grew gloomier still and fixed his two great eyes, otherwise employed for dignified looks, on an indifferent object, whose image painted itself on his retina to no avail.

In his own way, he cherished this dear child. By some miracle, she had grown into a pretty girl; her mother, who lay buried for ten years now, had been carried off by an aneurysm of respect.

People said that the poor woman had viewed her husband as something like Mount Sinai; finally, it had killed her.

Suzanne was luckier, for she had managed to make herself loved, more or less. As a consequence of inner movements that prove difficult to explain, the supercilious and hair-splitting Chaumontel had bowed before his daughter. Verily, the timber of his heart had softened for her alone. His condescension extended so far that he would suffer her caresses and indulge a few affectionate locutions or informal phrases . . .

And yet—I repeat—on that day, nothing worked. Chaumontel had reascended his column.

Suzanne gave up on eating, too. She put one of her arms around her father's neck and, in a voice that would have tamed wild apes, begged him to speak.

"You wouldn't understand, my child," he finally said in a somber tone.

Then, rising from the table like a man exhausted by bearing the weight of the world, he slowly withdrew without letting slip a further word.

Well, this is what had happened.

Two days earlier, Chaumontel had run into Bardache.

All the old derelicts knew Bardache—lanky Agenor Bardache, who had been sitting so pretty in the final years of the Second Empire, when he first started out.

In those faraway times, they had called him "the Parents' Peace of Mind" down on Rue Marbeuf. The queer individual had enjoyed eminent successes that a few senile men still recall. Illustrious personages lent him their support, and proud generals, tanned by the African skies, offered him rare garlands and nosegays.

After the Commune, which decorated him with several stripes, I believe, he disappeared to the antipodes for a few years.

The streets and sacred groves saw him again one day, but how he had changed! Now bearded, sallow, and grimy, he looked like a dried-out tree whose branches had grown too long. His angular face, plated with strangely livid spots, despite the powders and cosmetics he applied, called to mind the effigies of Evil without pardon sculpted so often in the Middle Ages under the feet of the saints, in the dark corners of basilicas.

Imaginative parties held that the paws of this muddy ghost were damp with the sweat of the dying, and everyone called him the Cadaver in the queer, pseudonymous milieu he frequented.

An altogether sinister particularity was that the joints of his bones cracked as he walked, as is said of Peter the Cruel.

Otherwise, he was as conspicuous as any appalling villain could be: he claimed to be employed as a business journalist and was seeking an advantageous marriage.

Chaumontel, pleased with himself and having just shaken honorable hands at the steps of the threshold of the First Civil Chamber of the Court, was about to mount in his carriage when this gutter-skimmer stopped him by touching his elbow in a gesture of familiarity.

"Well, then, my little *Deponent Verb*, don't you recognize your friends anymore?" asked the Cadaver.

With a gasp, the lawyer recoiled.

"But sir, who are you? I do not know you."

"You don't *recognize* me, my dear? Then I really have changed! But first, let's get into your hearse. I'll refresh your memory."

"Baptiste!" Chaumontel cried, "Go get a policeman right away!"

"Ah! Watch out, little *Deponent* of my heart! If you make a scene, I'll huff and I'll puff. I'll tell the police commissioner about our youthful hijinks, the little getaway in Marly and that room of heavy breathing where we had such fun. You could even take a peek at your photo; I bring it with me wherever I go . . . You know, the picture with you 'amongst the rosebuds to be gathered.' You offered it so kindly—since it was made for me alone—and inscribed a suggestive remark . . ."

At these words, Suzanne's father had grown quite pale. He abruptly called the coachman back; seeing that there were people watching, he himself ushered the horrifying companion destiny had sent into the car. He gave a quick command, and the team departed at full trot.

"So it's money you want?" he started.

"Money?" the other replied. "What do you take me for? I have the honor, Monsieur Chaumontel, of asking you for the hand of mademoiselle your daughter."

"My daughter's hand!" cried the defector from Sodom, full of paternal sentiment. "My daughter's hand! Are you going to smear my daughter's name with your filth now?"

"Come, come, dear friend, calm down—if you please, *let's be reasonable*! We're not children anymore, are we? We're not even young. The time of lovely follies has passed. I've lost all my looks, and every day I shed more feathers. I'm bored to death and hardly still alive. I'd like to become honorable—like you, my dear friend. For that, I need money, to be sure, but also a wife. It's natural enough that I thought of you, for you can give me the one as well as the other . . . Mademoiselle Suzanne is simply delicious.

" . . . Oh! Don't carry on like that; it's absolutely useless. Look. I've got your striking photo and, moreover, I have in my possession a few letters with which you once honored me; they are just as precious. I'll scratch your back if you scratch mine. You know what I mean . . . I'm giving you a month to get everything sorted—six weeks, tops. After that, the cat's out of the bag. I've got nothing to lose. Now have the driver stop. This is where I get out."

"Just one thing," stammered the unfortunate man, who had just tumbled down ten thousand steps. "You forget I can kill myself."

The other man exploded in laughter; from the running board he replied, "I'm not afraid of that. Pigs don't kill themselves."

The observation did not lack depth.

Two months after this exchange, Agenor Bardache married Suzanne in a village in Normandy where the lawyer owned an old house.

No one was invited, and the announcements (which Chaumontel had taken care of) were posted in the latrines.

The facts of the case are materially exact. Some other time, I'll tell you how the couple died. The father is still alive—thank God!

Ah! I forgot. On the wedding day, once the ceremony was over, Bardache, beaming, leaned over to his father-in-law and whispered tender words:

"Oh my friend, she's so much like you!"

XXIX. Jocasta on the Streets

Sanctum nihil est et ab inguine tutum.

JUVENAL, *Satire III*

Monsieur,

When this letter reaches you, I will surely be en route to Africa, where I will endeavor to get myself killed in an honorable fashion. If that may be called suicide, I think the manner is acceptable, even to a Catholic like yourself.

I am weary of living, I admit it—absolutely and irremediably tired of what the imbeciles and swine call "life" when they are among their own kind.

Please believe me when I affirm that my affairs are in order. I owe no one money, and no creditor will mourn me. My slight earnings, which I employed to no good end, will pass from me to pure hands.

I am without family, and my few friends and acquaintances hardly deserve a mention. My passing will not even be remarked, except by a lowly dog.

Before I vanish, however, I have decided to deliver to you a secret of terrible sadness and disgrace. I believe sharing it may prove useful to several people.

Let it be understood that you are entirely free to publish these *anonymous* words of confidence; unless, of course, your conscience judges it more prudent to destroy them.

Consigned to the post, this written confession will become as foreign to me as the unknown dramas slumbering in the limbo of a novelist's imagination. I have taken care that no one will be able to recognize me.

Do, then, sir, as you please. Here is my poem.

⚹

When I lost my mother at the age of six, I remember that my grief was intense—much greater, I suppose, than suits a child of that age, for I reaped an inordinate number of beatings for it.

I could never forget how it pierced and tore my tiny heart when I was cruelly informed that I would no longer see her; it was all over for my pretty mama: she had been planted in the ground, among the dead.

I was hardly able to understand what dying meant, yet I was oppressed by terror, crushed by horror, and never completely recovered.

The body wasn't shown to me. There was a reason, which I learned only much later . . .

Moreover, my bereavement was such that my father, a very hard man who loathed me, packed me off to the country the very same day—to the edge of a dark pine forest abutting a fetid pond and not far from a knackery; I can still see the sinister place before me now.

There I lived for two years, entirely deprived of culture, under the indifferent eyes of a desiccated peasant who fed me as meagerly as possible and left me to wander about all day long.

Poor little mama, among the dead! . . .

Often, I would stray near the killer's yard—drawn and dragged there as if by claws.

I could make out almost nothing through the fence, but I inhaled the place's abominable odor; I often saw enormous rats darting before me— hideous creatures that evidently came from the pond.

It occurred to me that she, my departed mother, had perhaps been put there, too—for already I sensed that the world is made in the repulsive image of that slaughterhouse, where butchers struck down suffering beasts.

Surely it moved God to pity when—and how many times!—I flung myself at the gate, sobbing and calling for my mother.

Ah! I was all alone in the world, let me tell you. I saw my father but once every three months, just for an afternoon. He would regale me with blows, for he thought me a juvenile idiot, an annoying little creep, and a young *thief* (!). He openly voiced the wish that, as he put it, I would soon "croak."

One day, I remember, he had mentioned taking a walk. And so he led me around the pond to a murky corner full of reeds, where I often spent hours on end staring at the swarms of tadpoles and salamanders.

All of a sudden, he barked the order for me to go pick a water lily floating a few steps away. As soon as I tried to obey the pitiless man, I realized in horror that I was sinking into the mud. Uttering blasphemies, he came and pulled me out when it reached my shoulders. If a witness had not come running when I cried in despair, I'm convinced he would have left me there—his face was diabolical!

Thus did I enter upon existence. I suppose you've had quite enough of my debuts. And so, I shall proceed to the years of misery that followed at the boarding school where my father had me locked up for the full course of two lustra.

Believe it if you can. Until I was eighteen, I didn't leave this prison for even a single day.

Naturally it would be pointless to try to make others (for whom childhood has held some joys) understand the necessary effect of such long and inhuman incarceration. It seems that civil law permits it—if I'm not mistaken, it's ancient *patria potestas*.

Fortunately or unfortunately, I was hearty enough not to die. For all that, I don't know what became of my soul in this cesspool. Ten years of contact with pupils and teachers would putrefy a bronze horse, as you know. A few writers have demonstrated as much to superabundance; I think it is useless to insist further.

There remained to me one single, precious thing, a kind of uniquely pure flower in a virgin corner of my plundered garden. This was the infinitely sweet memory of my mother.

A memory of delights, luminous and pacifying! Having lost her so young, I couldn't retrace the lineaments of her dear face, but I remembered her as ravishing, and the marvelous gentleness of her caresses was immortal.

The last time, to be sure, she had been so sad and so tender, my dearly beloved mother, so tender and so profoundly sad, that just thinking of it makes me melt in pity . . .

I am getting to the culmination of the story—which kills me, devours me whole, and defiles me beyond all conception.

When I got out of school, the man who called himself my father had aged so greatly I had difficulty recognizing him. He had grown, I should think, even more heinous.

His inexplicable hatred for me seemed to have worked itself up to a chronic rage it is difficult to describe; it called demonic possession to mind.

The first few nights at home, I barricaded myself in my room, fearing he would cut my throat as I lay sleeping. Such apprehension was childish, no doubt, but wholly justified by certain looks he would shoot at me on the sly.

He spoke few words—or none at all. *Our souls could see each other.* There was the sensation of standing face to face at the edge of a cliff.

He would bark a few brief orders—hard and cutting monosyllables. That was absolutely all.

It required no genius to detect that he had only had me return in order to inflict some new kind of torture. But I was now a man, I had learned from the shameful tribulations I endured at the boarding school, and I would have taken on even a young lion.

How could I foresee what has no name—the unspeakable horror the monster held in store for me?

He was an architect and commissioned with works of reasonable importance. And so, I was immediately assigned to run errands for a senior clerk who would initiate me into the art of building.

This individual—whom I carefully and very slowly *took care of* last week, before leaving Paris—was my father's confidant, the very soul of his damnation. I remembered that I had always seen him about the house. He had me work morning to night, without interruption.

When the first month was over, suddenly he played nice and informed me that his boss, who was not as tough I seemed to think, had decided to favor me with a reasonable stipend each month—even though I wanted for nothing under his roof.

"Well," he added, "everyone knows what young people are like. They need some fun after a hard day of work. Monsieur your father understands perfectly. I was even told to give you the key to the outside gate, so you can return at the hour of your liking when you go out at night. You shouldn't feel that you're a prisoner."

Naturally, the money this agent gave me—the first I had ever had!—softened my heart, and it no longer occurred to me to distrust him.

He promptly took full advantage and got all kinds of confidences out of me—which was not exactly a Herculean task, given that I was only eighteen and had no friend anywhere on earth.

He proved more and more easygoing and little by little became the chaperone of my corruption. He would get drunk with me and show me all the good spots.

I'll make quick work of the final episode. One day, the dreadful character—who *knew* what he was doing—gave me an address. No doubt, he had been holding it at the ready for just the right moment. He said it was for a woman who was "charming, if a bit ripe," who would fill me with delight.

Two hours later, *I slept with my mother*, who did not recognize me until the next morning.

Yours, etc.

XXX.   Cain's Luckiest Find

I don't know how, toward the end of a memorable dinner, such a height of stupidity had been reached that conversation turned to objects found on what is called, mysteriously and amphibologically, "the public thoroughfare."

Almost everyone in attendance seized the chance to recount tales of treasures lying in wait—saddlebags holding vast riches that had been stumbled upon; in these accounts, one cannot deny the dazzling selflessness of the actions performed. A few people, who weren't quite as drunk, lowered their heads and admitted they had never found anything.

And then, performing a grand gesture and summoning all the attention that lay dispersed, the stentorian sculptor Pelopidas Gacougnolle interpellated us:

"Do you know," he bellowed, "the lucky find Marchenoir made one day?"

The collective nutation of heads revealed that absolutely nothing was known.

"Well then, children, lend me your ears. The story's worth hearing."

"It is generally recognized," he began, "that our Grand Inquisitor of Letters was the most incomparable and calamitous youth ever to have dragged a shipwrecked frock or pantaloons upon our streets. Words cannot express the bounty of the dreamer's beggarliness.

"I remember seeing him many times during this epoch, and I'm so proud it's hard for me to believe the Earth can bear my weight! Oh! But I speak of a bygone age. I wasn't his friend yet, and I could hardly have guessed that I would be one day. I don't even know if he had any friends.

"He was a tempestuous and moody young razorback who only went slumming with the stars above. You could tell he had no patience for intercourse of any other kind; as far as I know, no one ever tried to win the savage over.

"Each of you knows him too well for me to wear myself out trying to describe him. Still, I'm not sure you can imagine him at eighteen, as he appears in a merciless portrait that he painted himself—in shark oil—and which he shows only to his closest friends.

"One sees him gnawing at his fist in compounded pitch, burnt umber, and lead carbonate; he stares at the observer with two terrible eyes bloodstreaked in intensity. If you haven't seen that, you haven't seen anything . . .

"Such was our hero's first style. He wanted to be a painter long before he felt himself a writer. Well! In his paintings, he would have been exactly what he is in his horrifying books: the silken mastiff and celestial cannibal we all admire.

"It's true: the eyes of this portrait, so haunting as to startle a virtuoso of my caliber, never cast the improbable gentleness the creator of volcanoes and lightning has kindled beneath his gloomy brow in order to confound imbeciles.

"Still, they capture an extraordinary resemblance, which even the most dauntless longevity cannot efface. They are the eyes of his soul—the true eyes of his deepest soul, eternally hungering for divine presentiments.

"Obviously, when he executed the exorbitant likeness, he had already been alerted—by the instinct of a man sequestered in the abyss—to his execrable destiny.

"Beyond all doubt, he had caught a whiff of the rotting carcasses that were to block his path, whose exhalations almost asphyxiated the three hundred lions he bore within him.

"How could he have failed to behold the vision of the infernal future—long since appointed, one must needs suppose—for his gladiatorial faculties? Indeed, I know of no man nature has so foreseen for black vipers and crushing vexation.

"Unfortunate souls who are not favored by such election should pronounce blessings, for he was—and still is—the rod that draws the lightning away from everyone else. For twenty years, he has presented a miracle: blaspheming the Rabble while remaining entirely invincible, upright in the saddle and braving the whirlwind of lowlifes and cyclone of cowards.

"Ah! What pride he may take in having been abandoned by the trusty gentlemen who called themselves his peers—whom he has seen flee, head over heels. The friendship, or even the simple admiration, he has been shown strikes me as something like the heavenly matches that only ignite 'on the box' (in the words the Septentrion has bestowed upon us).

"Heaven keep me from further lamentation on emotional agriculture and the political economy of cordiality. What is more, the man of whom I speak has made such definitive pronouncements that all rhetoric on the matter should henceforth prove idle. Each and every one of us knows the appalling inconvenience of not inhabiting a dog's hide when unkind destiny has refused us the snout of a contented swine . . .

"You will hear everywhere that this famously impecunious man has received the frenzied assistance of innumerable benefactors—indeed, that the innards of modern charity can scarcely be healed of the tumors his *ingratitude* has caused.

"He's held to have perpetrated his depredations in the world of letters above all. He'll gladly exploit even the grubbiest gigolo of the inkwell like a vein of diamonds, it is said. The calcified legend has grown positively incurable in the nether regions of journalistic secretion.

"I have taken care of a few of those stimulating valetudinarians—the sole of my boots refreshed their kidneys on the spot. Promptly, they recalled never having actually *met* the supposed affliction. On many occasions, Marchenoir has obtained miraculous cures in person. His methods, which surpass my own, are so infallible I consider him the greatest oculist of memoration—I'm convinced he could operate on the cataract of Niagara! . . ."

"But I'm getting carried away!" Pelopidas continued, taking his seat again. He had risen and, for a moment, was marching in great strides—knocking about this way and that.

"I simply lose my composure when I think of those beasts who would kill a man of the higher order just to glean three cents from the droppings left by the cynocephalous scribblers of the front page.

"Anyway, I was telling you I had caught a glimpse of Marchenoir during that distant age when he began his novitiate in the odyssey of famine and disaster. At the time, I was a pretty nasty little bugger myself. I slapped together little plasters and planted my own torso longitudinally on the street more often than I kneaded the clay of the academies. I was really wild—one of those clever rogues with tricks up the sleeve, given to dramatic hijinks. I might even have played dirty with this wretched individual; every now and then, one saw him pass in front of the workshop—rapturously deciphering some grubby scrap of print that looked like it was part of his ragged attire.

"But an instructive legend circulated about a certain no-good engraver whom, one day, he had precipitated into a puddle of mud *without even looking up from his book* and then hung out to dry on a window balustrade the sun assailed with its blinding arrows. The episode prompted reflection on my part.

"Anyway, however big a dunce I was in those days, the grandeur of such poverty had an effect on me. I detected the presence of an extraordinary soul; later, I understood that this was precisely what repelled the spawn of cockroaches crawling in our midst every time the strange wretch made an appearance.

"His rags, let me assure you, had nothing disgraceful about them. Indeed, the mangled fabric's cleanliness was curious and even touching.

"I can still see before me a certain towering hat—procured God knows how long ago! Its bizarre appearance is exceeded only by Thorvaldsen's unforgettable blunderbuss in that fresco bullied by the winds—the decrepit homage the Danes made outside his museum in Copenhagen.

"One saw this hat, which all the elements frequented, change as the seasons passed. It went through all the colors. The final state I had occasion to observe was the spiral, or snail shell, of Archimedes: the whitish convolutions made the wearer appear to be coiffed with a segment of spinal column wrenched from a collapsed basilica in Portugal; a few months later, this decisive phase was followed by an unmitigable sagging that three or four of the tougher guys in the workshop witnessed with great emotion. Words fail me when I try to express the care with which he used to scrub that undefinable object.

"After the catastrophe, he walked the streets bareheaded.

"I don't think he ever went barefoot, but the boots he wore made the sandals of the most stringent anchorites seem positively profane. Please give me leave not to expand on this point, or my poem will wind up as long as *Paradise Lost*; were I to dwell on secondary matters, it would dry us out as much as the evangelical prefaces to the end of the world.

"I cannot imagine the hyperbole necessary to provide a sense of the envelope that enclosed this aborigine of misfortune; many years removed, I picture the Cherub of Humiliation extending a claw to array his finery.

"Anyway, that's quite enough digression. Let me get back to my story."

"When I had the great joy, so long awaited, of becoming Marchenoir's friend and companion, I was, unfortunately, the powerless witness (for I wasn't rich then) of the indignities without name that an old landlady inflicted upon him.

"He owed several months' rent and could not manage, whatever he did, to satisfy her. The filthy woman wanted him to give her money at any cost.

"All the same, she kept him—but as one keeps pearl oysters in the fisheries of the Indian Ocean, under the constant supervision of watchful sharks. She had placed a most exacting embargo on the modest furnishings, already three-quarters destroyed, that came to him from his mother, and she always lay in wait for the chance to despoil him of any trifling godsends he might happen to receive.

"The unfortunate lodger was condemned never to exit his room except under the fire of complaints the fierce vulture launched. Several times a day, she heaped abuse on him in the presence of all the neighbors; often, she would assail him in the middle of the street.

"Messieurs, this situation lasted for ten years. At best, Marchenoir managed to pay in installments, and he could not resolve to flee. For the sum of three or four hundred francs, this wretched woman tortured him for forty seasons.

"Please don't be impatient, I'm getting to the point. What you have just heard was necessary to appreciate the unique significance of the find he made, 'that lovely morning of a summer so fair,' at the charming hour when the convolvulus and ranunculus of forest groves open their chalices.

"It had already been three years since the compassion of the Daughters of Ocean had finally unchained our Prometheus. A first literary success, bought at the price of torments inexpressible, had enabled him to cut the bands of ignominy. Now he was leading a reasonably quiet life in a solitary part of town—infinitely removed from the horrible gaol.

"The image of the female buzzard was growing dim, vanishing more and more into the fog—indiscernible, as if viewed through a telescope. It was impossible to find the negative, even in the deepest latrines of his memory.

"It was in July, almost at dawn, when the rising sun had barely announced itself. Marchenoir went out, as was his wont, to take the air on the city parapets and read a few pages of Saxo Grammaticus or Perotto's *Cornucopia*.

"He had taken some sixty paces and looked down at his feet while turning the corner. Two steps away—here, in this deserted location, where at the time stood only the fences of fruit gardens and unused lots—he happened upon a cardboard file most bureaucratic in kind, the sort belonging to an attorney or an officer of the court. Its presence astonished him.

"He drew close enough to touch it with his foot, and the object's resistance doubled his surprise—which promptly turned to horror when he saw a trickle of blood.

"He quickly removed the lid of the box, and *his landlady appeared to him* . . . The severed head of his old landlady was staring at him with dead eyes—dead, white eyes that looked like big, silver coins."

Erik Butler is a translator and cultural historian. His previous publications include *Regrowth: Seven Tales of Jewish Life Before, During, and After Nazi Occupation* (2011) by enigmatic Yiddish symbolist, Der Nister.